Fathers and Sons

To Barbara
and Dan
Family is everything

Witold Mierkedorn

WITOLD NIESLUCHOWSKI, M.D.

Fathers and Sons

Sonata Allegro

Chapel Hill Press

ISBN 978-1-59715-120-7

Library of Congress Catalog Number 2015907515

Printed in the United States of America

First Printing

Chapel Hill Press
1829 East Franklin Street, Building 700A
Chapel Hill, NC 27514
www.chapelhillpress.com

Cover photographs: (top) ©Halfdark/Fstop Images/Corbis; (bottom) ©iStock.com/roelofse.

Cover and text design by Michael Brady Design.

To Bonnie,
My wife, my first reader and first editor.

Sonata Allegro

1

"You can start warming up."

Dr. Jack Murano removed ice slush from around the heart. He didn't even have to turn around and look at his pump technician. Jack's operating room was kept cold and quiet except for the discrete oscillation of the cardiopulmonary bypass machine.

"Yes, sir, here we go," Ron answered. Jack had worked with Ron for at least twenty years and they knew well each other's likes and dislikes. They had to. In a time of patient crisis, communication should require only a few words. And Ron knew what to do.

All bypass anastomoses to the patient's heart were completed. The two proximal to the aorta could be done while warming up the patient.

"Can we have closing music?"

The final part of surgery was quite mechanical, so it was routine to play mellow, uplifting songs. Sometimes it was the anesthesiologist's prerogative to play the music during open heart surgery, but "closing time" selection belonged to Jack, so most of the time they played songs by Dan Fogelberg. Soon they heard *The Leader of the Band* from behind the anesthesia screen.

Quiet time in the OR was over, and two nurses sitting on their high stools during most of the procedure began talking about their past weekend's adventures.

Jack's mind, too, was free to roam.

He always wondered about the relationship between Dan Fogelberg and Dan's father. Were they close? How close? Did he teach his son to play music? To compose? As a cardiac surgeon, Jack had seen so many doctors in dysfunctional relationships with their children.

Family lives were sacrificed to advance doctors' professional careers. It was so easy to get lost in around-the-clock patient care. Doctors in hospitals were highly respected people, so all the systems were designed to help them deliver the best care to their patients. Teams of nurses and technicians were there to assist them and make their work easier.

After going home, however, wives and kids weren't so accommodating, and it was doctor's time to listen, not to be listened to. One incident stuck in Jack's mind. Saturday morning when he was not on call, Diane was out doing chores and he was getting the kids ready for a little party in the neighborhood. Jack didn't like their choice of clothes and let them know so. They looked at each other. "But that's the way we dress when Mom is with us." Jack still insisted they change. "We have to check with Mom," was their answer before they left to go to their rooms. "Really? My word is not enough?" Jack said, hurt, but he didn't show it.

After years of work, doctors' time spent in the hospital expanded naturally at the cost of their time left to spend with their wives and kids. Operating room demands often put a strain on family relationships with disastrous consequences. On the day of an anniversary or a birthday, many times surgeons, if they remembered, were buying presents in the hospital's gift shop. And when they didn't remember, well, the feelings of wives and children were hurt. It was bad enough for children to forget Father's Day, but the worst part was for wives not to feel they were part of doctors' lives. As a result, many of Jack's friends were divorced, and only a few of them had seen it coming.

"How are we doing?" Jack's mind was back in the operating room.

"Almost there, thirty-four degrees."

The patient's heart started beating on its own without the need for a defibrillator. Jack began hearing soft, distant beeps of the EKG monitor out of rhythm with the next song about Dan's meeting his old girlfriend on Christmas.

"Are we ready to come off?" Jack was ready to wean the patient off the cardiopulmonary bypass machine.

"Ready when you are," was Ron's answer.

Rick Burrow, the anesthesiologist, had his drips ready, but not much support was needed. They came off bypass smoothly with only minimal help from behind the anesthesia screen. Shortly tubes connecting the patient to the pump were out and drainage tubes in. It was time to close the chest. The PA would do it.

"Jack," Rick said, interrupting his train of thought, "he is a smoker and has quite bad COPD. I think he will do better after surgery with an epidural."

"Sure, it's an excellent idea." Rick was one of the best anesthesia people around. Jack knew that whenever he needed to be put to sleep, he would request that Rick do it. He had good judgment, excellent hands, and a quiet manner. It was nice to have him on the case. Epidural injection would not take a lot of time, and the delay of the start for the next patient would be minimal. Jack was already thinking of the next patient on the schedule.

"Tom, can you get the epidural tray ready for me? I will do it before extubation."

"Marcaine?"

"Sure."

"I'll get the tray and draw it to the syringe."

"Thanks, Tom."

Tom Bradbury was a CRNA and Rick's right hand in the operating room. He usually managed the patient on the cardiopulmonary bypass when Rick was taking a breather. Now it was time for Jack to have a cup of coffee, then talk to the patient's family.

Today's patient, Peter McCormick, was a local celebrity, a well-known business owner and a community leader. Jack knew him from hospital board meetings and had good rapport with him and his wife, Judy. Their kids were in many after-school activities together and their wives socialized often.

"Hi, Judy," Jack said to her and her sister in the small conference room next to the OR main waiting area. She was sitting in a nondescript hospital waiting-room chair with her knees together, hands resting on them, feet under the chair and body tilted forward. "How are you?"

"Nervous. How did it go?"

"Great, really no problems. Boring case," he smiled.

Judy relaxed and settled her back against the wall behind her.

"He is on his own, has only minimal bleeding, and we are giving him only a touch of dopamine. Just like we were discussing before surgery. You'll be able to see him in a couple of hours. The ICU nurses will let you know. Where are the kids?"

"Susan, my neighbor, dropped them at school and will pick them up, too. I doubt they will learn much at school today, though."

"Anything I can do for you, Judy?" Jack asked.

"No, thanks, you've done enough. I'll be OK here with my sister."

Jack went back to the doctor's lounge to await his next OR case. It was an uncomplicated chest surgery and he hoped to be home for a family dinner by six.

Dinners were respected events in Jack's household. Diane made sure everyone was ready and no one was interrupting. TV was off and the answering service was notified. Only the true emergencies were put through. Jack remembered that a few years after his arrival in the community, he and Diane were invited to a dinner at a prominent local neurologist's house. The host was on call for his group. The phone rang and Jack could hear the maid answering. "Yes, he is here, but he is at dinner and is not to be interrupted."

Will I ever be able to do that? Jack thought then. But he also knew that different medical specialties had different senses of urgency.

At home Diane and the kids were ready, looking proud to be able to keep such a seemingly simple routine going. Diane was a good cook, but for Jack it was the company that counted.

By the end of the family dinner the answering service called. *It better be important,* Jack thought. All nurses and operators knew how he cherished his time with the family.

"Doctor Murano, please."

"Speaking," Jack said.

"The nurse from ICU is on the line."

"Put her through, please."

"Doctor, your heart from this morning is stable and there is practically no bleeding. But he can't move his legs. It's already late and by this time he should be able to."

2

"Can't move his legs? Can he feel them?"

"No, he can't." Dara was an experienced nurse, another one whose judgment he could rely on. Her assessment was as good as his, and she had an advantage of being there and seeing the patient.

"Is he stable otherwise?"

"Yes, he is, no other problems."

"Let's wait another couple of hours and then reevaluate him. When do you finish your shift?"

"I just came in, so I will be the one to call you back."

"Please do."

Jack mind was running through the possibilities. Why can't he move his legs? Is this a residual effect of a long-acting anesthetic? Trauma during needle insertion? Aortic dissection? But let's wait. Let's don't worry about it yet. . . . Suddenly he felt warm and knew something was not right. He tried to read the paper, look at the news on his computer, then play solitaire. But his mind was at McCormick's bedside in the ICU.

In two hours Dara called again.

"Still the same, no change." The situation couldn't be managed over the phone any longer. It was time to see the patient.

"I am coming in, Dara," Jack told her.

The kids were already in their beds and Diane was reading. "I have to go and see Peter in ICU. He can't move his legs." Diane was used to his late-night escapades. She was a nurse herself and understood the intricacies of a surgeon's life. On his side, Jack could be sure that home was properly taken care of when he was gone.

Freeway traffic was pretty sparse, but Jack wasn't thinking of the road. *What else can it be? Am I missing something?*

ICU was quiet. The waiting room was empty long after visiting hours.

Peter McCormick was fully awake. Jack looked at the chest tube container. The bleeding was minimal. Urine output was good. There was sinus rhythm on the heart monitor. But Peter still could not move his legs, nor could he feel anything in them. Complete paralysis.

Jack called the OR. Usually in their hospital the anesthesiologist on call for a given day put the heart patient to sleep, so he expected Rick to be working in the OR that night.

"What are you guys doing? Are you busy?"

"Just a little trauma case," the circulating nurse said in answering the call.

"Is Dr. Burrow there? Can he talk?"

After a few seconds Rick picked up the phone. "What's up? Can't you sleep?"

"Rick, did you have any problems with today's epidural on McCormick?"

"Not at all, it all went well. Any problems?"

"Well, yes. He can't move his legs."

In the quiet on the other end, Jack could hear monitors beeping around Rick.

"It was just a thoracic epidural, not supposed to work all the way down," Rick explained. "And by now his legs should be back to normal." Pause. "Any possibilities of thoracic dissection?"

"No signs." Jack was looking at the chest X-ray.

"I wonder what can be a reason?" Rick was thinking aloud. "Nothing we can do at this point, anyhow. I think we should wait and see."

Jack agreed. "Let's evaluate him in the morning."

He went back to ICU again and saw McCormick. Still no change. Then Jack talked to Dara and told her about his conversation with Rick.

"I will keep an eye on him, Dr. Murano. Go home and get some sleep."

He knew he could rely on her.

On the way home Jack was numb, having no idea why Peter was paralyzed. His part of the surgery was uneventful, and he knew he could trust Rick. So what had happened? And what would he do now?

This was a rare complication of coronary bypass surgery. And how in the world would he break the news to Judy?

Suddenly he was looking at the world from a whole different perspective.

Andante accelerando

3

Peter McCormick had come from the East Coast, fitting into the community effortlessly from the beginning. Educated in North Carolina, Peter had inherited family money and moved to California some twenty years ago. He had bought a paper mill, and his business of making packing boxes for produce was booming. The area was heavy into agriculture, and the local farmers depended on him for supplying them with the containers for strawberries, broccoli, and cabbage.

His reputation was stellar; however, lately he was often seen at the local country club spending more and more time with a drink. He complained of problems with his workforce, compounded by a recent lack of water in California. On the other hand, his business was well managed and the farmers needed their boxes. The customers liked him, too, and Peter was taking care of their needs well.

Lately, however, more and more farms were closing. At meetings of the city council, there was talk of limiting water usage. This would be a death sentence to local agriculture, and Peter's business would suffer, too.

Peter's drinking didn't go unnoticed at home, either, and Judy was aware of his business tensions. He had also gained considerable weight. All this led to a visit to his primary physician, and ultimately he ended up on the operating table. Despite being overweight, his diabetes was well controlled and his prognosis for a recovery after surgery was excellent.

Not too many people knew that Peter had come from back East. Only his best friend and business partner, John Ortiz, had some idea. Peter didn't talk about it much and John didn't pry. All he knew was that Peter had been born and educated in Chapel Hill. And if one

9

was paying attention, he could detect Peter's residual North Carolina accent.

Judy, his wife, was from California. They had met there and married within the year. Twenty years and three kids later, life seemed to fall into a rut and become monotonous. Recently, however, problems with business were complicating his life to the point of putting a strain even on the relationship with his wife.

When Peter's drinking worsened, Judy confronted him. Peter finally opened up and she found out that alcohol was a real problem for him during his years in Chapel Hill, too. He quit then, but now, with all the work problems, he gained some weight, his diabetes got worse, and going back to drinking seemed temporarily to ease some of his pain.

During one of the social events at the club, he'd had chest pains and Judy insisted on his seeing their family doctor. Peter didn't pass the stress test, and after cardiac catheterization and a conversation with Jack, heart surgery was recommended. It came as a shock to Peter's entire family. The kids were devastated, but Judy's caretaker instinct took over and the entire family seemed to pull together. She felt somewhat guilty that circumstances had come to that, blaming herself for not seeing and not preventing this from happening. But she was determined to pull through it and soon became the family's stabilizing force.

4

The morning after surgery, having sent the children to school, Judy was getting ready to go to the hospital. Just then the phone rang. It was Jack.

"Judy, Peter had a good night and is stable. But I am sorry that I also have some bad news for you. He has no feeling in his legs and he can't move them. It's almost twenty-four hours and after any epidural all the functions should come back by now, but Peter has no improvement. We can't find a good reason for that, and all our tests are negative. We'll have a neurologist see him and of course keep an eye on him. Leg movement still can come back, but I am really concerned. I don't remember anything like this ever happening in my twenty years of practice."

A few minutes later, Judy was on her way to the hospital. Her entire daily schedule was turned upside down and she was rearranging her afternoon as she drove. As a mother of three, she was a master of multitasking and had been planning to see her husband in the ICU before noon anyhow.

Half-sitting, Peter was eating breakfast. His tubes were still in place, but the nurse said they would come out before noon. He felt no discomfort, but still couldn't feel his legs. Peter sat looking at his wife, not knowing what else to say.

"Has Jack been here yet?"

"Yes, he was, at six-thirty this morning," Peter said.

"Did he said anything?"

"Not much, just that he was concerned about my legs. They don't hurt, but I can't move them. And I can't feel anything from the waist down."

She didn't know what to say, but Judy didn't like it. Still she was hoping for a full recovery. The family had been planning a vacation as a part of Peter's convalescence. It looked, though, as if their meticulously organized trip might not happen after all if there was no improvement.

Jack came to see them between his cases but didn't offer much more than he already had during the morning conversation.

"We will have one of our neurologists come today and see what he has to offer," Jack said, trying to inject some hope but knowing, too, that chances for Peter's improvement were minimal.

Later that afternoon Judy was trying to explain everything to the children, but she didn't think they understood the implications. The youngest at five years, Mike was the closest to his father, and the boy's only question was, "When are we going to see him?" Later on John Ortiz called and got the bad news, too.

"Judy," he said, "don't worry, give him some time to recover. And in the meantime I'll take care of the shop. Peter was always a strong person."

"But what if he doesn't recover?" Judy said, expressing what everyone was thinking. The possible future of the household, family, and business all were racing through her mind. Could he still work? *Well, we are not there yet*, she thought, but the idea of being solely responsible for her family's well-being was overwhelming. *What if he is never able to work?* Judy thought. That would change everything. First the house would have to be redesigned or sold and a new one found with a different floor plan. Her already busy daily schedule would have to accommodate Peter's being at home. Would he need help? Probably yes, at least at the beginning. Would his personality change? What about his drinking? What would happen to their income and lifestyle, both of which she had so easily grown accustomed to?

Judy shook her head and made herself stop thinking about these dire possibilities.

She picked up the phone and called her sister.

"Sarah, Peter is paralyzed after surgery!"

"What in the world . . . ?"

"Jack doesn't know what to think about that and what to do. He hasn't had anything like this happen in his practice."

"Will Peter recover?"

"They have hope, but they are not sure."

Now Judy was getting angry.

5

Jack was beside himself. He tried to understand what had happened, but couldn't. Rick didn't have any idea, either. The anesthesiologist had contacted his mentor in the university where he was trained and also his good friends from that time, but nobody could help. Jack's two partners were also puzzled. Jack was still hoping that Peter's leg function would come back, but his knowledge of neurological injury in general didn't give him much hope. McCormick's paralysis was most probably permanent.

Jack's face-to-face conversation with Judy when he first explained what had happened was polite but a bit awkward. He could understand her apprehension. When with time Peter's condition did not change much and it was becoming more and more obvious that he might end up in a wheelchair, Judy was becoming reserved.

Then a chilling thought came to Jack. Is she going to sue? Friendship notwithstanding, she was becoming cold and distant, and what's worse, their contacts had slowed down to a trickle. Peter was transferred to a rehab unit, and Jack was seeing him only sporadically, at this point more as a friend than as his doctor. Visits weren't easy, but Jack was trying to put on a good face.

The idea of a lawsuit was coming into his mind more frequently. Then Diane told him that Judy hadn't greeted her in the grocery store. Their kids still played together, and Diane and Judy still attended school field trips. Obviously nothing of Peter's disability was discussed in front of either family's children.

The atmosphere in Jack's office was still pleasant, but it was not difficult to notice all the looks and halted conversations when Jack entered the room. Peter McCormick was a well-known and respected person in this town.

At this point Jack decided to contact Vance Schultz.

Vance was a local lawyer and a good friend. Jack and Vance had known each other ever since the latter had come to town. Vance had gone to law school in Chicago and was an avid hockey fan. He had season tickets to a local NHL club, and when his family didn't have time to go with him to the game, he often invited Jack. Eventually Jack learned how to watch the game and later on even began to like it. Long car trips in traffic to a hockey rink gave them another opportunity to talk and get to know each other. Jack went as far as enrolling his son, Luke, in a local ice hockey program for pee-wees, which at that time was quite unusual for a young child in California.

At Starbucks on Saturday morning, after hearing his friend's story, Vance tried to dispel Jack's worries. "Listen, Jack, she hasn't filed yet. And even if she does, I really don't see that they have a case. I don't see any causation. I can't tell you not to worry, but I do understand your initial reaction. We are not even close to any legal action now. She has, however, up to a year to file."

"It doesn't make me feel any better. And longer waiting feels like hell."

In the following months Jack had a feeling of a sword hanging over his neck. Work had become almost mechanical. He took no joy in doing surgery anymore. When others were congratulating him on a case well done, his answer was, "I'll feel good when the patient goes home without complications." Even at home his interaction with Diane was cooler, more superficial. No more laughing and no more picnics at a local winery. The children were still young and didn't sense anything wrong, but for Diane the change was palpable.

One night, when the kids were asleep, she cried, telling Jack, "I hope it won't get any worse, because I don't know how much more of this I can take."

After three months it became obvious that Peter's leg function would not improve. Judy arranged for a basic house remodeling to accommodate the wheelchair, after which Peter was able to move back home. Business was being taken care of, at least temporarily, by John Ortiz, but at home the situation was different.

Every activity taken for granted before surgery had now become a chore. Daily personal care had to be planned ahead and took incredibly long. Dressing needed to be assisted. The same with washing and bathing. And this was just a beginning. The house had to be fitted with a stairlift. Meals took longer. There was no office work anymore, but this only left more time for Peter to mull over his current situation. He was slowly adjusting to his new arrangement; still, the mental load was overwhelming. Peter was spending more and more time on his computer, taking care of his photo library.

However, when no one was at home, Peter visited the liquor cabinet more frequently. He had problems with time management, was napping during the day and spending nights on the Internet. He was in need of new interests, yet he was finding none. All his friends were working, so his attempts to contact them were unsuccessful. They had no extra time to spend with Peter. His old, active life had dropped away from him, and the new world forming around him was narrowly circumscribed.

Judy didn't handle the new situation well, either, and was becoming restless and angry. She was the one stuck with the most of the family responsibilities and chores. On top of the usual school activities, childcare and managing their household, she had now become the main caretaker for her paraplegic husband.

Her elderly parents lived within a one-hour drive, and since her brother lived far away and her sister, Sarah, had a full-time job, by default she was also taking care of them.

No, Judy didn't like it a bit.

6

This afternoon Jack was seeing patients in his office. The day was long, but follow-up visits were usually rewarding. It was nice to see them relieved and healthier after surgery and compare their present health with how they felt when he saw them first. But so many things had to go right to have the expected good results. That was just one of the intricate truths of a surgeon's life.

His first patient was Mrs. Black, whom he had known for years. He had done a heart surgery on her years ago and now, with poor weight and diabetes control, the procedure had to be repeated. There were problems with her daughter coming from out of town to help, and he had to send a letter to her employer. Also her dog, with whom she never parted, had to be boarded, and Jack's office staff would have to help. And all this had to be done even before surgery was scheduled.

The next patient was Mr. Contreras, who after heart surgery had to be seen by a hematologist. When the patient called the hematologist's office himself, the scheduling assistant gave him the first available open spot—in three months. It was not acceptable, so Jack picked up the phone and by talking to the doctor was able to make it happen the very next week.

Jack felt strongly that his patients were owed his undivided attention, so staff was requested not to interrupt him with minor problems, even though he was bombarded continually. For him it was a sign of respect, the same as dressing properly and addressing the patients by their last names. He could never bring himself to call Mrs. Black "Betty," which came naturally to young girls from the front office. He cringed each time hearing that, but after a while he just gave up. Today, however, during Mr. Contreras's visit, he was interrupted when the nurse told him of a new arrival to the ER of a patient who needed his immediate attention. He excused himself, left the examining room, and called the hospital.

Sometimes Jack thought of himself as being in the business of problem solving in addition to being a doctor. He was confronting major and minor problems all his professional life, and everyone expected him just to solve them. Many of them came even before a patient was on the operating table. His entire training had been designed to condition him just *for* that.

Then he came home. Diane was quiet and felt down. After a while spent waiting for her to open up, Jack asked, "What's happened?"

"It's our principal again. She doesn't want our kids to participate in travel team sports. She . . ."

"I can talk to her," Jack interrupted.

"She doesn't feel," Diane continued, "they are strong enough academically to be able to catch up with the loss of so many classes."

"We can take their books with us, have extra assignments, and do homework on road trips in the car." Jack had many solutions to the problem.

"I asked for that and she still refuses. I don't think she likes our kids. Is she . . ."

Diane was again interrupted. "Let me talk to her. I'll take care of it. I'll help you!"

Diane looked at him. "Jack, I don't need your help. I just want you to listen to me. And I hate you interrupting," she told him with fire in her eyes.

A master in his medical kingdom, at home he was still learning.

7

Jack had always wanted to be a cardiologist, but then he realized that surgeons saw results of their work quicker and the treatment process was usually more dynamic. He felt that surgeons always dramatically influence people's lives, mostly for better but sometimes not. Those failed cases—and the fear of cases failing—were the most difficult and put enormous pressure on Jack.

Cardiac surgeons responded to stress in a whole variety of ways, and Jack had seen all of them. Some surgeons coped by remaining aloof, impenetrable, rough, and even mean, and at the other extreme some prayed with their patients and their families before surgery. The former didn't accept blame for any complications, and nothing that happened was their fault. The latter seemed able to absorb much more stress and tolerated it easier, at least as far as one could see.

Jack fit somewhere in between. He was known occasionally to pray before a tough case and never had fits of rage during a major mishap in the OR. Rage and tantrums, in his view, were not only inappropriate but didn't help and, moreover, didn't make any sense. His calm demeanor was not the norm, however. Cardiac surgeons were known to have enormous egos. Oddly, their willful blindness to the reality of justified blame helped some of them to deal with the pressures of their profession.

A story had circulated about Denton Cooley, the famous Houston-based surgeon and innovator, a gifted man. While testifying in court, Dr. Cooley was asked by the opposing attorney if he considered himself to be the best heart surgeon in the world.

"Yes, I do," was the answer.

"Don't you think that a little immodest, doctor?" the smirking lawyer asked.

"Sure," answered Cooley, "but remember, you put me under oath."

Jack's mentor, a well-known cardiac surgeon and Renaissance man, the author of many professional books and publications, was asked one time which books he was reading.

"I don't read," he replied. "If you write them, you don't have to read them."

After Peter McCormick's ill-fated surgery, however, all had changed in Jack's relationship to his work. First he noticed that after three or four hours of sleep, he was waking up and couldn't go back to sleep. The big digital clock at his bedside glared at him in red and he couldn't wait for six o'clock, his usual start of the day. One night he had a nightmare of driving his car into a deep sandy ditch. Walls of earth started falling down around and on top of him, and he found himself buried in dark, dank mushy sand with no possibility of opening the car door. He couldn't breathe and woke up in a sweat with his heart racing, knowing that another day ahead would be blighted by his lack of peaceful sleep.

His unease started to show in his guardedness at his office and in the operating room, and soon he sensed that people were talking behind his back. If Jack had been highly disciplined and terse before, now he was as stern and vigilant as a sentinel primed for enemy attack. His personality changes were also clearly visible at home. One night, during a bedroom conversation with her husband, Diane cried out, "I want my old Jack back! You are too cruel to yourself—and through that to me."

But things were not moving in that direction, the right direction.

8

One morning, Holly, Jack's office manager, stuck her head in.

"I just got today's mail, and there is a letter for you. You'll want to open it yourself."

Looking at the return address, he noticed "Esq." after the name. The letter from an unfamiliar attorney requested a meeting to discuss problems concerning care of Peter McCormick. He also requested copies of Peter's medical records from Jack's office.

Jack immediately contacted Vance Schultz.

"Don't meet him and don't send him any records," Vance told him. "You must notify your insurance company. And for goodness sake, don't change any of your chart notes!"

It was not a formal letter of intent to sue, but Jack knew that was coming. At home, despite bad news Jack and Diane had a feeling of partial relief because they'd been expecting this to happen. At least there was no more waiting for the ax to fall.

After a few weeks and no response from Jack, the next, more official letter came. "This is to notify you of our intention. . . ." He didn't have to read the rest. He knew.

First was the meeting with the handler from Jack's medical malpractice company, then a request for records that would be sent to an expert from the local university. These legal steps were predictable, but very slow and methodical. He knew he was in for a long reckoning—the ax would fall slowly, but fall it would.

Jack had been sued before in a couple of minor cases and one strange, frivolous one. This time, however, the litigant was prominent, and his action brought against Jack hurt the most. And last but not least was the feeling that his malpractice insurance rate, high already, was going to be even higher—with or without a guilty verdict. *They don't really have a case*, Jack thought. *Nothing within my control happened to Peter to justify this complaint.* But he also knew that that didn't matter.

Somehow the news of the lawsuit got around, and even the local paper mentioned it on the front page. Phrases like "botched surgery" and "local businessman damaged for life" hurt. Jack wanted to stand up and scream, "That's not my fault!" but he knew no one would listen. He has been labeled for life. And even if and when he was exonerated, not one reader would care when the paper printed a small mention on the last page in barely visible print—if that.

So Jack got ready for a long process of legal wrangling. Every detail of his medical life would be scrutinized. Every decision undertaken under stress in the operating room would be second-guessed by lawyers and expert witnesses in their plush offices. They would have the luxury of changing and editing their opinions. All *his* decisions were final, however—no second chances. And in the view of the community, Jack saw that he was already guilty.

He looked out the window of his office. Clouds were gathering in the high, blue sky of sunny Southern California.

9

Jack Murano, a cardiovascular surgeon practicing in a group with two other partners, was well-known in his community of close to two hundred thousand. His ancestors had come from Italy, and he always cherished his cultural roots, even learning to speak Italian for his fre-

quent trips to the old country. Jack was fascinated and puzzled by the
magnificent culture established by the Romans during just a few hundred years two thousand years ago. He also admired the ability of the
Italian people to live full lives despite all the drama surrounding them
through the centuries. Learning of and enjoying their rich historical
and cultural heritage was a treat for him and an excellent counterbalance to his busy surgical practice.

Out of all places he had seen in Italy, Assisi was his favorite. One
of many hilltop towns in that nation, its ambience was quite different
from the others. He felt something profoundly spiritual while visiting
the Basilica of Saint Francis. Crowds were always enormous but well
behaved, respecting the sanctity of that holy place.

This was the year of another planned trip to Italy for Jack and Diane. Moreover, they needed at least a temporary distraction after the
lawsuit had been filed, so they chose the serenity of Umbria.

The Muranos usually stayed in an agriturismo in Orvieto and
rented a car to travel. One could drive almost anywhere and be back
for dinner. There were no deadlines, no pressure. And the best adventure was to get lost in the countryside. Occasionally one could
find hidden treasure like a lonely monastery and be invited inside by
a monk to have a sometimes not-so-simple meal with him. Even better was to meet him and his brother-priests.

A day after arrival, Jack and Diane took a short drive to the home
of Saint Francis. It was the middle of the week, so crowds were not
bad. They walked up to the Basilica of Santa Chiara among groups
of tourists and Catholic nuns. There were also groups of young priests
eager to show them the way around and describe surrounding trea-
sures. Diane wanted to buy a ceramic piece from nearby Deruta for
her budding Italian collection and was trying to compare the prices.

On the way to Basilica they stopped at the coffee shop they fre-
quented whenever visiting Assisi. A little table on the patio outside
had a spectacular view of the surrounding valley. The beauty of this
place was remarkable. Jack observed the folded mountain chains; the
closer ones were greener, those farther away were gray. Jack smiled,
remembering his grade-school teacher as she tried to explain to them
how the light and distance worked.

Diane took a picture of him sitting alone at a small table, drinking
cappuccino and reading a local paper. He texted it to Rick Burrow

with a note "Breakfast of Champions." It was an ongoing joke between them, with a poking "na na na na na nah" added. Rick was probably busy in the operating room at that moment anyway. The idea for this picture came from a photo Jack had found on the Internet. On a crowded Italian piazza a young man dressed in an elegant suit sits alone at a small table drinking his first cappuccino and reading the paper. That image represented a cool, elegant, and effortless time management or *sprezzatura*, and Jack loved it!

At the next table they overheard English spoken. After a short introduction, it turned out that the man was an ex-pat teaching English at the Universita per Stranieri, in neighboring Perugia. He had been born in Chapel Hill and educated at Duke. Kevin had left the United States as a result of his disagreement with the direction the country was going. Italy seemed a perfect place to him, and its relaxed lifestyle fit him well. His companion was a young woman studying design—also in Perugia. Their conversation was lively, and they both kept politics out of it.

Then was Jack's turn to tell about himself. After hearing where he was from, Kevin opened his eyes wide and smiled.

"I know this place. My mother lives there."

"Really!" said Jack. "The world is so small."

Kevin's mother was a resident in a local retirement community, a source of many of Jack's patients. He visited there from time to time. Initially, when he first came to the community, he was planning to give lectures in a large conference room for eager retirees in order to introduce himself to possible future patients; later on he paid occasional home visits to several of them.

"Well, so what are you doing here?"

Jack gave Kevin his name and said he was a heart surgeon on vacation.

The professor got quiet and looked at Jack. "So you were the one who operated on Peter McCormick." Jack stiffened, his smile disappearing as he looked at the ex-pat. Then he turned to Diane and leaned back against the chair. With both hands he began to rub his forehead. All the surrounding beauty had disappeared for him. *Halfway around the world?* he thought. *And still no release from blame!*

"Yes, that's me. And how did you know about that?"

"I keep in touch with my mother and read your local paper."

Conversation fell off as they all appeared uncomfortable. Diane collected her things, ready to leave.

Kevin said, "So how well do you know Peter?"

"Just as his doctor. And our wives and kids have quite a few after-school activities together. We used to be friends," Jack said with a dry smile. "Now, as you know, he is suing me. How do *you* know him?"

"We went to the same school in Chapel Hill." Kevin looked directly at Jack. Was he gauging the effect? "But you probably didn't hear about the car accident he caused, did you?"

Jack and Diane looked at each other in disbelief. This was getting really interesting.

A group of noisy schoolchildren was passing by, their teacher trying desperately to get them in order but to no avail. They were showing her small souvenirs from their visit to the Basilica and all were talking at the same time. Jack and Diane looked at each other; they had expected to get away here from the turmoil in California. Once the group of children moved on, Jack saw no reason to leave, and soon the ex-pat professor had Jack and Diane's undivided attention.

10

"Peter was born to quite a wealthy family," Kevin began. "They have been in Chapel Hill as long as I can remember. His grandfather was a tobacco farmer, but his father foresaw a business decline and sold the land. Peter's father had degrees in pharmacy and an MBA from Duke, becoming a high-profile executive in one of the local pharmacological companies. Peter, following family tradition, was accepted at Duke after sensing that his father wanted him to go there.

"An interesting father-son relationship had emerged in his family. The father was a high achiever. Peter, on the other hand, had always felt that he would never measure up to his father's successes. He loved and admired his father, but when he was comparing their accomplishments and interests at the same age, there was a visible gap.

"In the McCormick family, college was obligatory and Duke was the only good choice. But Peter's time in the first two years was evenly split between the classroom and the fraternity activities, and later on he gave even more weight to the latter. Beer drinking was very popular on campus, and Peter was not known for retiring early. He was also playing lacrosse at Duke, but still found plenty of time to socialize.

"Famous and infamous parties were held in Pittsboro, a few miles south on Route 15-501, not far away from his father's house in the Governor's Club. This two-lane road was heavily used by bikers, with multiple signs warning motorists, 'Watch for bicycles' and 'Share the road' as well as yellow and black signs of bikers posted on roadsides. Also several memorials for fallen bikers stood with their twisted, broken cycles painted white and left forever attached to the road signs in the wide median divider. Yet on this dark, open road barely anyone was expected to drive at or below the speed limit.

"One wintery late Friday evening Peter was driving from one party in Chapel Hill to another one in Pittsboro. The stretch right north of Fearrington Village was open though the lighting was minimal."

Jack looked at Kevin with furrowed brow. "How do you know all those details? Sounds like you were there."

"The passenger in Peter's car was also a friend of mine." Kevin took a sip of coffee.

"It was easy to lean on the gas pedal and enjoy the car's speed. The boys were animated and alcohol was making them both feel invincible. As a result, Peter didn't notice the lone biker riding at the right side of the road despite his bright fluorescent vest. When he did, it was too late. The tires screeched, and the biker flew off the road from the terrific impact.

"Peter didn't run. Police and ambulance were notified immediately. Unfortunately, however, his blood-alcohol level was well above the limit and charges were filed against him.

"I don't remember the biker's name. He survived but spent a long time in the intensive care. There were many operations and a long rehab period. After he finished his treatment, he ended up paralyzed from the waist down.

"The trial was quick, but it divided the community. Peter got off on technicalities: the police on the scene didn't do their job properly, the evidence wasn't preserved correctly, and the highly paid criminal attorney from Charlotte did the rest. Then all the rumors quieted down.

"Shortly thereafter Peter vanished from the Triangle. Then I've heard of him from my mother, who says he's living in the same community as is she. We weren't that good friends to begin with and I didn't keep up with him. I never contacted him, so we never spoke with each other. Nothing in particular, I just didn't have a reason. But that's the story as I know it."

It was quiet at the small café table despite crowds walking past toward the Basilica. Jack and Diane regarded each other for a few seconds. Finally she said softly with a slight head tilt to the side and her eyes wide open: "Karma?"

The rest of their stay in Umbria was overshadowed by these revelations, and soon the Muranos were eager to get home.

11

After returning from Italy, it was back to the everyday grind for Jack in the office and in OR. Doing surgery had been a good counterbalance to the pressure of his everyday life. But not now, for he thought constantly of the lingering lawsuit. A few months ago, too, right after McCormick's surgery, Jack noticed that he was hesitant to start any new case.

Each incision he made on a new patient reminded him of the possibility of a terrible complication. His throat went dry, he stiffened up, and he thought, *What is happening to me? Why am I doing this?* This feeling were so damaging to his confidence that he couldn't enjoy the intellectual or the creative challenges of being a surgeon. None of the usual fun in the OR came to him anymore. It was so bad that Jack often couldn't wait to get home from the hospital.

After some time, though, the office seemed to run a little smoother, though on Vance's request he still couldn't open up about the case with his partners. The only ones he could talk to were his wife and, of course, Vance Schultz. Vance was fascinated when Jack told him Kevin's story from Assisi. He didn't believe in karma, but his legal detective mind was working overtime.

"It would be interesting to find out the possible connection between these two cases," Vance said, offering Jack his help. "It so happens I am going to Raleigh to take a deposition in one of my cases. I'll take one or two more days off and see what I can find out." He would take care of his practice for a few days by long distance from the East Coast.

12

RDU airport was a huge contrast to LAX. It was spacious and modern, and the crowds of Los Angeles were three thousand miles away. The next-day's deposition proceedings in a rented office at one of the local hotels was lengthy, but Vance still had time to visit a large gray building in downtown Raleigh where local newspaper offices were located and asked to see their archives. They were closing shortly, but he was permitted to come back and continue work on his project the next day.

It didn't take much time to find out the name of the victim. Since the accident had happened in Chatham County in 1978, the trial was assigned to a court in Pittsboro. In the time left, he decided to drive to Pittsboro. He took 15-501 south just to have a feel for the road. The ride carried him through North Carolina's "enchanted forest," as retirees from the North called their new abundance of greenery. He had to be careful, though. Cops were everywhere and the speed limit was strictly enforced. He found the courthouse right in the middle of a large roundabout with a statue of a Confederate soldier standing guard with rifle in front of the access to the monument of justice. The building where the archives were located was just behind. He found out where to come back to the next morning.

A few minutes before closing, the guard was still there.

After introducing himself, Vance was told that a few years before, a fire in the courthouse burned up most of the archives. People were joking, the guard said, that the reason for the fire was that sex tapes of a former Senate candidate and local politician were stored there. Fortunately, copies of all courtroom files were kept in the neighboring Siler City as well. This could mean another trip for Vance. But at least he was on the trail.

The next day he was back in Raleigh at the *News & Observer* working on putting all the pieces together. It took awhile, but Vance was spellbound by what he was learning and barely found time to take a coffee break.

When he came in, Vance began talking with the receptionist. She was a middle-aged woman, and her voice told him she had been born in North Carolina. He introduced himself and mentioned what he was here for. Oh sure, she remembered the trial, but the details were fuzzy. "But you could ask Ray McBean," she said. "He is the oldest one around and, I reckon, was a fresh news reporter when that case went to trial." She was kind and showed him the way to the requested files.

Vance found Ray's room on the second floor, but the reporter was in the field, giving Vance enough time to go back and sift through the archives.

The name of the biker Peter hit was Colin Bradbury. At that time he lived in a small condo in Fearrington Village and quite often commuted to work in Chapel Hill on a bike, working as a research lab assistant there. While riding back one evening from his work, he was hit by a car driven by Peter McCormick. He survived, but his spine was severed. Bradbury spent weeks in ICU and months in rehab.

Peter's trial was short. He had stopped and called for an ambulance. This was a mitigating circumstance. Shoddy work done by police and investigators on the scene was mercilessly exploited by a prominent personal injury attorney from Charlotte, so Peter got off with probation.

There were rumors, however, that after the trial some money had changed hands, but again no proof of that appeared in the local paper. Colin was able to buy a nice house in Fearrington Village and use their excellent Duke rehab. The accident and its consequences put a significant strain on his marriage, though, and he and his wife divorced. She took both of their kids and moved to Charlotte, where she went to work in a bank.

Of Colin's two children, a boy and a girl, Tom was the one really close to his father. He was interested in sports, and his father was at his side all the time. The boy started with baseball and in high school somehow got interested in lacrosse, always hoping to be accepted to the stellar program at Duke. The fact that his father was a Duke alumnus was a great help.

McBean's secretary called, and Vance returned to Ray's office. Waiting in the reception area, he saw pictures of governors, senators, and college basketball coaches—all signed. Ray McBean appeared to be well embedded in the community. Shortly the reporter came in and again Vance introduced himself.

"So, what can I do you for, counselor?" McBean sat in his chair with his legs extended and the fingers of both hands steepled in front of his chest. He looked in charge. "Of course I remember," he said after the lawyer explained the reason for his visit. "I was a young news reporter in this case and earning my stripes there."

Vance told him briefly what he had learned from the official police reports found in the archives in his visit to the courthouse and from old newspapers in his own building. Then it was time for the reporter's recollections.

"Twenty years ago this was a small community and everybody was fascinated by the drama. There was a general feeling of disappointment when McCormick got probation, but not much could be done at that point. And not much was done. The obvious irregularities in police work stood out, and the presented evidence to convict was very weak. On top of it, Colin Bradbury had no money for an appeal and the whole thing was dropped.

"One thing I was struck by while watching the entire trial, though, was an incredible bond between Bradbury and his children. Particularly between him and his son, Tom. For a few days the mother brought both teenagers to the courtroom. They were nicely dressed and well behaved in the midst of the great commotion of that high-profile, traumatic trial. They seemed overwhelmed with all the uniforms, procedures, and occasional banging of the gavel by the judge. And to top it off, there was their father in a wheelchair, the view of which they still had trouble getting used to. Tom rarely took his eyes off his father, but when McCormick was testifying, little Tom pierced him with his gaze, his body bent forward. The boy looked as if he was ready to jump over the wooden railing off the gallery.

"Yes, there were rumors of payoff, but nothing official. Then McCormick disappeared, and with time things quieted down."

"How is Bradbury doing? Is he still around?" Vance asked.

"Glad you asked. He lives in Fearrington Village, has a house there. They have an excellent rehab center there, too, and he uses it to the fullest."

"I would like to talk to him. How can I find him?" Vance found a trail he could follow.

"Sure." But McBean was in a hurry for his next appointment. "They have an office in the Village Center and they'll direct you from there." Vance got up, thanked Ray, and left the office.

Once down in the lobby, he grabbed a sandwich in the coffee shop and found his car. *Roads in North Carolina are sure well maintained*, he thought, while driving 15-501 about six miles to Fearrington. Was it just north of here that Colin was hit on the way home that night?

Vance found Bradbury at the Galloway Ridge rehab center, a part of Fearrington Village. A trainer on desk duty showed him the pool where Colin was exercising. "His session with Jerry will end in fifteen minutes." Finally the chair pulled Colin up from the water on a mini lift. A technician situated him on the wheelchair and dried him off.

Vance introduced himself and asked if Bradbury would be willing to talk about the accident.

"It's an old story," Colin said while being helped to dress and change to a dry wheelchair. "But sure, we can talk," was the answer. "I can meet you in a little cafeteria next door. It's only for residents, but you can tell them you are waiting for me."

Bradbury wheeled himself to the cafeteria with the energy of a long-distance competitor. His upper body was well developed and clearly visible through a thin T-shirt. It looked as though the hours in a gym over the years had served him well. Vance introduced himself again and made a casual comment about the magnificent facility Colin had.

"It's well situated," was the answer, "and keeps me competitive. That's still left from my basketball days. So tell me again, what brought you from the left to the right coast?"

Vance told him that he was working with a doctor who recently operated on Peter McCormick. The operation had ended with a significant complication and the surgeon was now being sued by McCormick's family.

"And how did you find me?"

Vance continued with the story about Jack's trip to Italy and the ex-pat he had met in Assisi.

Colin seemed comfortable talking about the accident and his problems following that tragic event, and Vance was eager to find out as many details as possible. He described to Vance the hours and the days before and after the event, including the memorable Friday he worked late to finalize an overdue project.

"It was dark already, and my wife was at a school activities meeting and couldn't pick me up. So I had to take my bike. The ride downhill on Franklin Street was wonderful, and when I joined 15-501 it was a straight shot down to Fearrington. The road was empty and quiet. When I passed the Harris-Teeter grocery store, though, I noticed headlights coming up behind me. The car was going from side to side and was obviously speeding. I tried to move off to the right side of the road, but it was too late. I heard an ear-splitting shriek of braking tires and felt a horrendous hit from the behind. And then I felt nothing."

Colin woke up from a drug-induced coma two weeks later in ICU, still on the ventilator. A few days later, the breathing tube came out, and he was able to talk. The drains from his chest came out next, but the feeding tube was still in his stomach. Both leg fractures were pinned, but he could not feel them. He was told that his spinal cord had been completely transected by fractured spinal bodies and he would never be able to walk again. He was still hoping then, but hope vanished quickly and all his will was poured into his maintenance of a healthy lifestyle and exercising of his upper body. He bought a new home, but Vance didn't pry into how he got the money. The strain on the family was immense, though. His wife and children moved to Charlotte. "The hardest thing for me was to part with Tom, my son, but not for long. He came to study in Chapel Hill, and we saw each other often. That went a long way toward giving me something to live for."

Colin asked about Peter.

Vance told him about his mishap during the surgery.

"So where is he now?" Colin was visibly interested.

"In California," Vance explained.

"In California?" Which town? Which hospital? After Vance gave him the details, though, Colin turned silent and looked away, seeming to have no more interest in their conversation.

But Vance had gotten what he wanted. He met Bradbury, heard his side of the story, and in a few hours he was on the plane to LAX.

He couldn't wait to tell Jack what he'd learned.

13

Litigation was gradually putting even more stress on Jack's life. News of the "botched surgery" on a community leader had spread like wildfire during a hot season in California. Diane was as supportive as possible, trying to take his mind off the legal and social nightmare. His closest friends were also trying to cheer him up, joking with him and reminding how a good surgeon he was. "Every surgeon has complications," one of them said. "Some have more than others, but you certainly are at the bottom of that list." Jack acknowledged and appreciated it, but reminded them that "they don't listen to character witnesses in medical malpractice trials."

Their social life suffered, too. Jack couldn't quell his perception that everyone wanted to ask him questions about "bungled" surgery. Besides his not sleeping well in the weeks after, work in the operating room and seeing his patients in his office became dreadful chores. The first few cases after Peter's surgery were a nightmare to start. Later on he was able to concentrate better, but his gun-shyness before the first incisions never went away.

His referral practice also suffered. He noticed that he was seeing fewer and fewer patients, and cardiologists weren't asking him for consultations as often as before. He wondered if these were patients' own decisions or their doctors'. The results, however, were the same, and his productivity declined. He had an agreement with his partners to split the office overhead and income equally, but certainly this would change if his patient load continued to drop. *Thank God all this didn't filter down to the children's level,* Jack thought, and they did continue to socialize with Peter's children without any questions being asked.

Every quarter Jack and his two partners had a business meeting in the office. They met promptly at 7 a.m., before the rest of their work was under way. Meetings were run by Larry, their business manager, who had an MBA. Coffee and doughnuts started the day on the right foot. One of the secretaries had recently resigned, and interviews with new candidates needed to be set up. Also a contract proposal from the new insurance company had to be reviewed and acted upon.

But the main point of the presentation were Larry's financial reports. They were prepared in a standard accounting form of profit and loss. All pertinent data were allocated to a particular surgeon, including number of patients seen in the office, patients seen in the hospital, and the number and type of operations. Listed was also income from other sources, like reading studies from the ultrasound laboratory, ER call reimbursement, and so on.

Jack's numbers didn't look good. He was seeing fewer patients, did fewer surgeries, and his general productivity was down. This had rarely happened to him in the past, and never to this degree. He couldn't look his partners in the eye. Nothing was being said, but he felt the uneasiness in the room. Income was still distributed equally after this meeting, but a discrepancy in the workload was now clearly visible.

Not that he was not willing to work, nor did he take more time off. Jack didn't know what to do about his production gap. He knew, however, the reason for it and was frustrated, since he couldn't do much. His partners obviously were aware of his problems, but they said nothing—yet.

Could they refer some cases to him to equalize the patient load? Probably they could, but it would be impractical. These patients were sent to them by the other physicians or on the patient's request, so giving away these cases would not be fair to the wishes of either group. So there was nothing to be done. It was becoming clear to Jack that the discrepancy in his bringing income to their corporation would soon force a different formula for compensation. This would mean less money and certainly a change in lifestyle for Diane and the kids. There'd be fewer vacations, and their planned house remodeling would have to be postponed. He saw significant changes coming.

Social interactions were another story. Some of his close friends were very supportive, and it showed in their conversations. But kindness was not universal. Quite a few others avoided him, and some even were giving him "the look." He also met with a few hostile remarks that he felt weren't deserved. When Jack entered the dining room in the doctors' lounge, conversations often went silent and restarted after a short break. Many times they didn't include him at all. He felt ostracized and frankly didn't know what to do about it.

In the past he had read stories about professional and financial death. Was this what he was slowly experiencing? It was not that he was not getting *any* referrals. But the patients he was getting now were so sick that doing surgery on them almost guaranteed complications and bad results, leaving him with a miserable track record. All healthier and better-risk patients were landing under his partners' care.

On the other side, Jack was getting more emergency cases, which often had higher complication rates, not to mention that most of them came after hours. And nothing spreads in the medical community faster than news about complications during and after surgery. Such news was the great horror they all feared.

So Jack was put in a situation he couldn't win. He felt stymied, boxed in. Not only was there no light at the end of the tunnel; there was no tunnel, no opportunity at all. He couldn't take it any longer.

Something had to give.

14

Vance came back to California on Friday, and the next day he was sitting with Jack in Starbucks. Though still early morning, the place was humming with people trying to catch up on news from the past week.

"What a different world they live in in North Carolina!" Vance started. "Lots of green spaces, excellent roads—well maintained and with little traffic. And people try to help you a lot."

Then he told the story of the accident twenty years ago he had found out about in the Pittsboro courthouse archives, from the *N&O* reporter, and finally from Colin himself, the paraplegic victim of Peter's car accident.

"So what was his name, Vance?"

"Whose name?" Vance seemed back in a different time zone.

"The guy from the gym, you know, who Peter hit?"

"Bradbury, Colin Bradbury. He has quite an arrangement over there. A bucolic yet sophisticated area to live in and a house with all the accommodations for a wheelchair. And a nearby gym is a big help to his health, too. Excellent facility. All the trainers have degrees in physiotherapy." Then he thought for a while. "But I am sure he would give the world not to be forced to use it under these circumstances." Vance took another sip of his coffee and looked out through the window at a father playing with his son in perfect California weather. Then he turned to Jack.

"But do you know what he told me he missed the most?"

Jack looked at him expectantly.

"He told me he missed not being able to be with and travel with his children while they were growing up. That time has been lost forever. That's his biggest regret."

They sat for a while in silence. Outside the young father took his son's hand and they walked to the car. Jack was watching them. Then his brow furrowed and he massaged his forehead with is fingers.

"What was this paraplegic guy's name again?"

"Bradbury, Colin Bradbury."

"Bradbury? This name sounds so familiar. But I can't attach it to a face." And the Saturday crowd and noise were distracting.

Then his mind drifted to the ever-nagging problem of his lawsuit.

"Vance, what's next with our case? Any movement there?"

"I found a good expert witness for us. He's a recently retired cardiac surgeon from UCLA, and he's agreed to review the records. I told him briefly about Peter's problem, and he didn't think they have a case. But of course he needs to see your office and hospital charts. He will also need your deposition. It may take some time. And how are *you* doing, Jack?"

"I am managing a little better. I can work OK, but my patient load is still down. I'm really worrying about being able to support Diane and kids. I hope that'll change, though it's not going to change on its own, is it?"

On the way home he was thinking of the name Colin Bradbury. Then something came to him. Recently there'd been a going-away party for a CRNA working with him on heart cases. He knew the guy, only his first name was Tom. Wasn't his last name also Bradbury?

The next day between his OR cases, Jack caught up with Rick. "Yes, Tom's last name is Bradbury. As a matter of fact, he was helping us during Peter's operation. His father was sick and needed help, so Tom went home to help him out."

After his last case Jack went down to the medical staff office. He was a member of the surgical committee and had access to all medical staff files. His good friend Clara was the director of the department.

"Sure, here they are," she said, handing him a binder with "Thomas Bradbury" on it. "He recently resigned his staff privileges, and we're in the process of closing his file."

Jack went to sit in the conference room to look through the bound stack of documents.

"Thomas Bradbury, born in Chapel Hill, N.C., graduated from Chapel Hill in 1988 and got his CRNA credentials from Duke University in 1992."

One of the best schools in the country, impeccable credentials, Jack thought while thumbing through the recommendation letters and periodic performance review notes. No filed complaints and no disciplinary actions. A picture-perfect record.

"Where is he now?" he asked Clara.

"He just moved to Chapel Hill. His father is sick and needs help."

Incredible, Jack thought. Another North Carolina connection. So what had happened in Chapel Hill in the past? And are these events related? Is Tom's father illness somehow tied up to events in California? All these questions started popping up in Jack's head. Jack was surprised not only to see a tunnel but also a dim light at the end of it. The McCormick case revealed itself to be far more complicated than anyone around Jack Murano would imagined.

The key of his music piece was changing from minor to major.

15

Jack had just finished giving his deposition at a huge office building in downtown L.A. After seven hours he was completely drained. Vance joined him in a coffee shop downstairs.

"Well, how do you feel?" he smiled, looking at Jack.

"So tired I'm not even hungry anymore . . . So how did we do?"

"You did fine. They tried to put you to sleep with routine simple questions and then trick you with a sneaky one. Except for one time, you stayed on balance and most importantly didn't take it personally. When you were describing your operating procedure, though, you didn't have to describe and explain so much. Doctors have a tendency to justify their actions and often get themselves in trouble that way—by being ego-driven and defensive. No one likes that, so just answer their questions. The other guys are just waiting for that. They train for getting a rise out of you.

"And one more thing. Your emotional answer to their last question, 'How do you feel about Peter ending up paraplegic?' may have even helped you."

"But it is the way I feel. I am really sorry."

"I am glad you didn't blame it on anybody else."

"There is nobody to blame it on."

Jack took another sip of coffee, trying to recollect the details of his deposition during the answers when he was especially on guard not to fall into a "gotcha" moment. He wished he could go back and give some of the answers differently, but it was too late now. Somehow the good answers were coming to him well after the fact, when he couldn't do a darn thing about it. Well, this deposition was a memorable experience, for good or ill.

"So what's next for us, Vance? Do they have an expert witness yet?"

"I still don't know. One way or another they had to have input from a medical professional before your deposition, just to know what questions to ask. And as you know, some of them were quite pointed. I'll let you know when I have the name. So far they don't have a probable cause. And they don't even know the mechanism of Peter's injury. They are treating and charging you as the 'captain of the ship.'"

Jack smiled. The "captain of the ship" doctrine was designed to keep a surgeon in the operating room legally responsible not only for his actions but also for the actions of all other people present during the time the patient is there. He is in charge. He gets all the glory, but he's also blamed if something goes wrong.

It was a cold day for LA, and Vance was cradling his coffee cup, buried in his thoughts.

"Jack," he asked, "do you have any idea what had happened that day in the operating room?"

"Have no idea. Not only that but neither does anybody I could talk to. It's a complete mystery as far as I am concerned." Musing a little, he focused on a barely visible speck on the wall. "But you know, Vance, certain ties sound intriguing. There could be something there. That CRNA working on our surgery with Peter has the same last name as the guy paralyzed by Peter in the Chapel Hill accident. And they all grew up in the same area."

"Really! How did you find out?"

"I spoke with Rick, my anesthesiologist on this case. He is not working with us anymore."

"Rick?"

"No, Tom Bradbury. The CRNA."

"Very interesting. Are these Bradburys related?"

"I need to find him and talk to him."

Vance looked at him and slightly turned his bowed head from side to side, implying, *Oh no, where is he going with all that?*

16

At home, dinner was ready, and Diane had a lot of questions.

"Why do we have to go through all of that?"

"That's a part of the system. Everybody has a right to have his day in court," Jack said.

"But what about all those frivolous suits?"

"They are also a part of the system," he said, laughing wryly.

"Besides the huge emotional impact, all this increases the costs to the public and raises your malpractice insurance rates. Even when you win!" Diane was not giving up.

Since kids were staying with their friends, at least the two could talk freely. Jack was thinking about this day's OR cases. Diane was watching her plate.

"How come they always find lawyers to take unjustified, frivolous cases?" she asked, relentlessly. "They just clog up the courts, slowing the legitimate progress of justice for the rest of us!"

"They do. And you know what? They will always find an expert witness to testify for them. It's up to the judge to throw out the obvious, outrageous claims and the jury to sift through the details of the others, if the case gets that far. It still costs a lot of money and time. You are very right about that."

They ate in silence, Jack thinking of his deposition, Diane of the many complexities of the legal system.

"Do you know what I just found out?"

Diane looked up.

"What?"

"The CRNA who helped us on Peter's case has the same last name as this man who was hit by Peter's car in Chapel Hill some twenty years ago."

"No way! Can that be just a coincidence?"

"I really don't know. But the CRNA quit right after that, so he isn't working with us anymore."

After a moment of quiet, Diane looked at him and knew there was something else.

"And he is from Chapel Hill, too," Jack said.

17

Diane stopped eating and pushed her plate away.

"Really!" She looked at him with an expression of incredulity. "How did you find that out?"

"I have access to his personnel file. Since he left, they are in the process of closing it."

"What was his reason for quitting?"

"He had to go to Chapel Hill to attend to his sick father."

"And what do you think of that?"

"I'm not sure, but it would be reasonable to talk to him. If he only wants to see me . . . But before that I need to talk to Vance."

Jack met Vance in his office the next day after work.

"I doubt he will agree to see you," Vance said. "But if he does, he may not without his lawyer being present in the room."

They were quiet for a moment.

"Do you think he can add anything to this case? And if so, will he be willing to?" Vance asked.

"I don't know, but I would be very curious to find out. I am running out of possibilities and have no idea what happened in my operating room that day and why."

Another pause.

"I have to find a way to get in touch with Tom Bradbury," Jack concluded.

18

The next day Jack was doing a case in the OR with Rick. After surgery was over they spoke in the recovery room.

"Do you remember the CRNA who used to work with you? He was also on that case with Peter McCormick."

"Sure I do. Quite a capable young man. Why?"

"He was born and educated in Chapel Hill."

"So?"

"Peter McCormick was also born and educated in Chapel Hill." Jack looked at Rick, watching his reaction. "What did you think of him?"

"Good, smart worker. Always on time. Very disciplined, but kind of a loner. Didn't have many friends." Rick looked startled. "Do you think he could have anything to do with what happened to Peter during the surgery?"

Jack was not ready to answer. "Rick, how do you do your epidurals?"

"This one, as far as I remember, was done while Peter was asleep. The CRNA usually gets the tray ready when we position the patient on his side. Then I prep his back. Didn't have to use local anesthetic since the patient was still asleep. I put the needle in and inject a few ccs of marcaine."

"Did you draw the liquid yourself?"

"I usually do, but Tom offered to do it for me. I remember we were busy at the time and didn't want to delay the next case."

Some commotion in the large room signaled that the patient was being taken to recover after surgery. A crew of nurses and technicians was checking the blood pressure, attaching him to the breathing machine and connecting IV tubes.

"Doctor Burrow, your next patient is ready in the pre-op area," the intercom announced.

"Got to go, friend," Rick told Jack.

"I have to talk to him," Jack replied, half to himself.

Jack found Clara in her office.

"Could I see this file on Bradbury again?" She pulled a reddish folder from the file cabinet.

"What are you looking for, Jack?"

"How do you guys get in touch with him if you need to?"

"Here is his cell number and the email address. Most likely he didn't change them."

Clara knew everything about everybody. She was perfect for her job. "What's going on, Jack?"

He smiled. "You will be first to know. Well, maybe the second."

They were good friends.

Jack was home earlier than usual. His surgeries were done, and he had no office time this afternoon. Diane was getting ready to pick up the kids from school.

"You're home!" It was a simple statement, but Jack felt it as a judgment for not having more patients and not working hard enough. Even at home he couldn't get away from his overwhelming feeling of generalized guilt.

"I spoke with Rick, and he remembers the case. He didn't draw marcaine into the syringe for Peter's epidural himself. Bradbury offered to do it for him."

Diane looked at him, then said, "Where are you going with all this?"

"Rick remembered that there was a broken-off vial capping the tip of the syringe, but he didn't remember if he read the label. They were busy."

"And where were you?"

"I was out of the room. My part was over, and the PA was closing the chest."

Diane's phone rang. She looked at the number and didn't answer.

"For all of that, Rick said he really didn't know what he injected during the epidural."

"What if he injected poison?" Diane's nursing background was coming into play here.

"He certainly could have. Peter was under anesthesia, so he couldn't feel anything." Jack looked at his wife with admiration. He was often finding new reasons why he'd married her.

"In any case, I need to find him and have a little conversation about this case. Vance said that Bradbury may not want to see me, though, at least without his attorney present."

"How are you going to make him talk?"

"Not sure yet, but first I have to give him a chance of refusal. Oh, I almost forgot. Vance called. We have our expert's opinion. He saw only a few minor mistakes, but nothing substantial. He didn't think I went below the standard of care. He also thinks that the 'captain of the ship' doctrine will not hold up in court, and thus they have no case."

Diane looked at him, smiling slightly, then shook her head a couple of times and gave Jack a brief hug before grabbing her keys and purse.

"I gotta go."

19

"So you think Tom Bradbury had something to do with it?" Vance looked at Jack, who was warming up from his coffee. For California it was unusually cold and windy, and people were seeking shelter.

"I'm not holding my breath, but I have to start somewhere. This case is disrupting my medical practice and ruining my finances. I certainly hope it's not going to ruin my family life."

"And how are *you* holding on?" Vance was the only person besides Diane with whom Jack could talk openly.

"I will tell you how, Vance. After it became obvious that Peter would be paralyzed permanently, I didn't even want to get up in the morning. Even so, I had to go in, see the patients, do surgeries, go to the meetings. I'd never known what gun-shyness means. Diane tried to help, bless her heart, but really couldn't."

Jack bent over the table and looked into his friend's eyes.

"Vance, did you ever watch *Dr. Kildare*? No? I grew up on them. I was in medical school and watched them religiously. They were so good that even as a medical student I was able to learn something new from each. In one segment Jim Kildare meets another doctor. He is a primary physician, but after a while it becomes obvious that he sends most of his patients for 'consultation' or 'second opinion' to the other physicians. The volume of consultations seems a little excessive to Jim, and he mentions that to his mentor, Dr. Gillespie, who is also a director of the hospital. After some hesitation Dr. Gillespie tells Kildare the other doctor's story.

"He made a minor mistake and ended up with a lawsuit. He didn't take it well, his drinking got worse, and he nearly lost his practice. His wife almost left him, too, unable to tolerate his mental changes. She couldn't understand that he was ready to throw away all those years of learning and practice.

"But Gillespie saw that this doctor was afraid to make any decisions on how to treat his patients and was using other doctors as a crutch. It took an accident with a pedestrian hit by a truck to turn him around when he, as a passerby, saved the unfortunate man's life.

This got him out of the doldrums. He realized that he still had skills and still could be useful as a doctor."

It was quiet except for an espresso machine buzzing in the background. The wind outside had quieted down, and for some reason only a few people were left in the shop.

Jack looked at his friend's eyes.

"Vance, I am still waiting for a case like that."

Vance was listening without saying a word, nodding slightly. He seemed to understand what Jack was going through. Then after a short pause, Jack said, "I called Bradbury and left him a message. I also emailed him."

"Jack," Vance answered, "if he had anything to do with all this, he will not talk to you and you cannot force him to testify. At least not with your state of knowledge about what happened that morning." Vance was clearly after a solid, realistic legal strategy.

"I can ask him a question, though, and see what he has to say. First he has to answer my email."

20

Friday afternoon after the office and one minor case in the OR, Jack went home. The kids were back from school, and Diane was sitting in the kitchen, reading the morning paper. The TV was on—another fire in California. The pictures were spectacular, flames shooting high and embers flying all over. Fortunately the scene was a barely inhabited area of the forest and no houses were in danger. But Jack felt like his own house was on fire.

"We had a business meeting in our office this morning," Jack said, sitting down across from Diane.

"OK?" She kept reading. The kids were playing in their room upstairs.

"Diane, I'm not doing so well with my productivity. The third quarter in the row, mine is significantly lower. It was mentioned in today's meeting for the first time, but I expect soon something will have to be done."

Diane put the paper away and turned off the TV.

"What do you mean?"

"Well, they might want to change the percentages of reimbursement from the partnership funds."

"How are they going to do it?" Diane was frowning. It wasn't good news.

"So far we were splitting money equally, but with me working less and bringing in less money, they will ask for a change in the formula. Probably the overhead still will be divided equally, but the rest will be based on productivity. It means less money for us."

Jack was trying not to sound alarmed, but Diane knew better. She was the one spending their money when Jack was working. It would be easy to cut and economize daily expenses initially, but if the trend continued, their entire estate plan would have to be changed. College plans would have to be reevaluated, vacation plans redone. Diane was thrifty with groceries and clothing, but she knew there was only so much she could do to limit spending.

"Can we stay in the same house?" she asked cautiously, perhaps not wanting to stir up his anger. But it was a big question that would have to be asked. Their emergency fund was there but not as large as they would like.

"Nothing was said yet, but if nothing changes, no doubt they will ask for a revision of the partnership agreement."

Another moment of quiet settled over the table.

"You know we have plane tickets to this wedding on the East Coast? They are expecting us."

Diane's niece was getting married. As a godmother to the girl, Diane could not skip the celebration.

"What can we do to trim our expenses?" Jack was not very familiar with household budgeting.

"Well, I am using coupons already, getting gas from Costco, shopping for the kids' clothes at Target. All my clothes are bought on sale. We could eat out less. A new car for me can wait, but school is coming and that's another huge expense."

Jack was looking at his wife, deep in thought.

"Jack, do you think we'll have to move out of our house?"

But as soon as the words were out of her mouth, she turned the TV back on. Diane didn't want to go any further into this conversation.

The fire was still raging in the California forest, reminding Jack how quickly things can go up in flames.

21

Bradbury's email read, "Of course I remember you well. It was nice working with you. I really have nothing to say about this case, though. Take care, Tom Bradbury."

Jack didn't know what to think about the email. Diane, however, had an idea.

"First of all, he did answer. He didn't have to. He still may want to talk to you. If he did have anything to do with Peter's problem, it's very human to need to talk to someone about it. Most 'perfect' crimes are solved that way. People want to brag—or confess—about their accomplishments. I wouldn't let it go, Jack."

Jack wasn't convinced. For him it was another setback. Then he thought for a while. There was nothing to lose in pursuing Bradbury. And he'd learned already he was never wrong to rely on his wife's judgment.

After a moment of hesitation, he sat at the computer and sent another email to North Carolina.

Later on at the office, he looked at his schedule for the next day. First on the list was the case he'd been thinking about for a while. It was quite a complex procedure involving heart valves and coronary arteries. The patient was sick, his heart was weak, and the technical part of the procedure probably would be difficult. The chances for complications were high. He used to do even most complex surgeries with his PA, but after Peter's case, he didn't feel quite comfortable enough to operate without backup. There was a high probability something could go wrong, and he felt that the PA's hands may not be enough. He was not in the position to take any complications at this time. Jack took out his cell phone and pressed his partner's number.

"Hey, Carl. Jack here. What are you doing tomorrow morning? Are you busy?"

"I have two minor cases to do in the outpatient surgery center. What's up?"

"I have a double valve with coronaries to do tomorrow and may need your help. Will you have time? I'll need you maybe for the two hours we'll be on the bypass."

There was quiet at the other end. Carl knew that Jack used to do these operations with just the PA's help. He didn't really need anybody else. Jack was a capable surgeon, well organized, and he didn't make many mistakes. He made no unnecessary movements, either. Jack had no emotional ups and downs during the procedure, no OR drama for which other surgeons were well known: many even cultivated a bad-boy behavior. He liked to go in and out of the operating room smoothly and efficiently, and the staff loved him for that. But now it was more and more obvious that Jack had changed. He needed a crutch to do his work.

"Sure I can help. I'll ask the front desk to reschedule those two cases. No problem."

But it *was* a problem, though, and everybody knew it. Jack was becoming visibly more cautious and apprehensive. His risk tolerance was low, and mentally he wasn't solving complex problems well. His decision-making process, so important in this field of work, was greatly impaired.

Jack expected he would not sleep well tonight—and tomorrow he would no doubt need extra coffee. But at least had secured his partner to help for the next day.

22

Jack didn't sleep after 3 a.m., just tossed and turned. He welcomed the alarm at six and was in the OR at seven. It took two cups of coffee just to get him started. The patient's family was waiting, and he requested extra time to talk with them. A volunteer took them to the conference room, since he didn't want to discuss the intricacies of the case in front of their father. He again explained the reason for surgery and described what he was planning to do. Jack also talked about the complexity of the operation and the poor condition of the patient's heart.

"However, the surgery is the only way to help him," Jack explained, "and not doing it may shorten his life. At the same time, the remaining quality of his life would be miserable. I hope you understand and accept the possibility of complications. It's not pleasant to hear that, I know, but I also know you want to hear the truth. From my side I will do everything in my power to get him through that."

Their faces were somber. They thanked Jack and said that they had full confidence in him.

Jack had covered all the bases.

On the way to the doctor's lounge, he stopped again and talked to the patient. In the lounge, Jack drank another two cups of coffee. The other surgeons were coming in one by one. Jack sat in the corner club chair and silently prayed to be able to overcome all foreseen and unforeseen difficulties during the surgery.

The patient was put to sleep in OR 5, Jack's usual room. Today's anesthesiologist was John Green, with whom Jack wasn't as comfortable in working on big cases as he was with Rick. He requested Rick, but Rick had been assigned to a different case a while ago and couldn't change. Jack would have to deal with it. It took longer for John to put all the lines in, and that gave Jack time to have another coffee.

He started the operation with his PA, who harvested the vein from the patient's leg while Jack was making preparations for cannulation and connecting the heart to the cardiopulmonary bypass machine.

"Dr. Stone is here. Should we ask him to scrub?" The circulating nurse had answered the wall phone.

"A few more minutes, we just gave heparin," Jack answered. The vein was harvested and the incision on the patient's leg closed.

Carl joined them at the operating table.

The patient's heart didn't look that great. With the thick layer of fat on the surface, it was contracting slowly, deliberately, having great difficulties pushing blood through the diseased valves.

"Let's have the intraaortic balloon pump in the room, just in case." Jack was preparing for possible difficulties after coming off the bypass. "And please stop the music. I want to have complete quiet this morning."

Jack and Carl worked efficiently around the heart. No one was talking. The staff sensed the severity of the case and the possibility of complications.

They did the coronaries first, then one valve and then the next one. Pump time was long, but Jack thought he'd protected the heart muscle well with proper cold solution and ice slush around it. It was time to warm up the patient and come off the bypass machine.

"Carl, I think I'll be OK now. Thanks for coming."

"Are you sure? Let me stick around for a while. I'll be in the doctor's lounge. Just in case."

"Thanks again, Carl."

Jack was on his own.

"Are we warm enough?"

"Yes, thirty-six degrees," Ron said, on top of it.

"Ready to come off?"

"Ready when you are. Here we go."

Jack clamped the tubes going to the heart and saw it slowly filling up with blood from the pump. He was watching his patient gradually taking over from the machine.

"Do you have all your drips ready?" Jack asked the anesthesiologist.

"Yep, we are ready," was John's answer.

They were slowing the machine down, but the heart was failing, not ready to take over.

"Let's go back on the bypass. And maximize all the drips," Jack ordered.

They waited for another fifteen minutes and tried again. Again the heart pumped for a while but then got larger and again failed. Jack was becoming uneasy. He noticed that his hands were shaking. Was it stress or too much coffee? Or both?

"Get me an intraaortic balloon ready." They went back on bypass. The heart was not taking over. It was going to be a long afternoon.

"Do you want me to call Dr. Stone back?" The circulating nurse asked, trying to help.

"No, I think I will be fine." Jack didn't want the drama of his assistant being called back to help him. Soon he would have entire OR staff peeking through the windows.

The balloon was in and they tried to come off again. Slowly the patient was weaned off the machine. Jack kept the tubes in, just in case. The heart was paced by the wires attached to the external pacemaker. This was synchronized with the work of the aortic balloon. The drips were maximized, so the patient would get the full support. Still, the patient's heart looked like it was working very hard.

Jack was getting hot, and his own heart was beating fast. He noticed his hands were getting sweaty, too, despite the cold temperature in the room. They felt slimy under his surgical gloves. He didn't remember feeling like that for a long time.

"Let's wait before we close." Jack was emotionally and physically exhausted and asked the nurse for a stool while he waited. He looked at the EKG monitor. There were too many extra beats, not what he wanted to see after the heart operation.

The operating room was quiet—no music, no one taking breaks. Everyone was sensing that the patient's life was hanging on a thread. Jack was thinking, *Is he going to make it, or is it juſt the calm before the ſtorm?* It looked good so far, but the surgery was not over yet. He waited for another fifteen minutes, then removed the cannulas from the heart. Jack sat again on his stool, waiting, with the chest still open. The heart monitor was still showing many extra beats. Not a good sign. The blood pressure was steady, but borderline. Not much bleeding, though. This was the encouraging sign. Jack was not ready to close the chest yet. The quiet in the OR was deafening.

Is this case ever going to end? Jack was at the end of his cool.

And then it happened. The EKG monitor showed a high zigzag burst of heart fibrillation. Jack jumped up. "Charge the defibrillator!" It took two shocks to stop it, but the shocks also stopped the heart. "Pacer on!" John Green was working furiously behind the anesthesia screen. "Max the drips!" But the patient's blood pressure was down to sixty. *I am going to lose him*, was screaming in Jack's head, but he still was able to control himself. Then another burst of ventricular fibrillation, and after another shock, the man's blood pressure fell to thirty. "We are going back on the bypass!"

"Stitch!" Jack yelled to the scrub nurse.

"Not that one, aortic!"

Jack stomped his leg twice on the floor and threw the instrument across the room, after which the nurse quietly complied.

This had never happened before. Jack had never lost his temper in the operating room. In a few minutes they were connected to the machine again. Jack wanted to give his patient's heart some rest and then try again, but it didn't work. Then more rest and Jack tried again. Still no results. One more time. This time longer. Everybody in the room was watching Jack, who felt enormous pressure not to let the patient go. No one more than he wanted the patient to survive. He waited longer, but the man's chances for survival were getting slimmer every minute.

This patient is dead, came to Jack's mind. He couldn't get him off the bypass machine. There was nothing else he could do to save him.

He went around the table, stood in front of John Green, and yelled, "You killed this patient!" His finger was pointing to the anesthesiologist's chest. Then he slowly walked to the corner of the room; methodically removed his gown, gloves; and mask; threw them on the ground; and left the operating room.

The room was quiet.

Jack went to the lounge and poured himself a cup of coffee. His hands were shaking and his mind was racing. The prospect of talking to the family was sickening to him. There was no way to explain what had happened, no way of expressing his sorrow. He would wait for a moment. He needed to gather himself while he designed some kind of strategy. How was he going to face the patient's family? Was there any way to describe what had just happened? Then a voice from the intercom shook him again like a jolt from the defibrillator.

"Dr. Murano, you are needed in OR 5, stat!"

What now? What do they ſtill need me for in this miserable room?

Jack jumped and ran back to his operating room. He regarded his team and noticed everyone was busy. The monitor showed blood pressure of one hundred and a nice EKG of the heart properly paced by an external pacemaker. The patient was alive. *How did it happen? How did they do it? They brought him back when I was out in the doctors' lounge drinking coffee! I'd given up on him,* Jack thought. He was embarrassed and humiliated at the same time. An unbelievable thing had happened, but he knew stories like that had happened in the past.

He looked at his team. No one was looking at him. They were all busy working, seemingly ignoring his presence. At this moment he even wasn't a factor in a surgery listed under his name. The ship was sailing through Scylla and Charybdis, and the captain had left his bridge. When he was in his quarters, the crew had led the vessel into the calm waters—all when he was sitting in a big, comfortable chair drinking coffee. Would they want to work with him in the future? Would he ever be able to regain their trust?

He scrubbed again and rejoined the team. In complete silence he finished the operation and closed the chest himself. Then he stood up in the middle of the room.

"I am really sorry for my behavior today. This has never happened in the past and will never happen in the future. You guys did a magnificent job, and I will never be able to repay you for that. Again, I am very, very sorry." Jack spoke to everyone but was looking primarily at John Green.

Then he left the room.

23

"Vance, how are we doing with our case?" Jack had called him, since he hadn't hear from Vance in a while.

"OK, I guess. Not much from the other side. Still haven't heard from their expert witness, so they may not have one. I am sure they had some medical advice, though, judging from the questions being asked during your deposition. But they still have to find the doctor to formulate an opinion and be able to defend it before the jury. The first is easier; the second may be more difficult. I still don't think they have a case, and during the motion for a summary judgment, the judge may be able to throw entire thing out."

Jack smiled wryly. "That's your wishful thinking."

"In law, as in medicine, there are no sure outcomes. You should know that. That's where judgment comes into play. My own long experience tells me that any case they present wouldn't be strong at all. And that's my best judgment, Jack."

"Vance, I have other news." There was silence on the other end.

"OK?"

"I got an email from Bradbury."

"Really! What does he have to say?"

"Not much. Just that it was nice working with me but he has nothing to say about the case."

"But he answered your email."

"Right. That's what Diane focused on, too." Another pause.

"And what do you want to do?"

"Diane told me not to give up but try to talk to him."

"She is a smart girl."

"Yes, I know. Vance, I'll somehow have to go find him and talk to him."

"If you want to. Let's talk about it soon."

Days went by with nothing exciting at home or in the office. Jack sensed that something was brewing. And then another message came from North Carolina.

The email read, "I am presently in Wrightsville Beach and will be there for the next several days. If you decide to come here, call me when you arrive. Tom Bradbury."

Jack rescheduled his office patients and surgeries and booked a redeye for the following night. Then he went on the Internet and checked on Bluetooth microphones that could be paired with his iPhone. He found one that could easily fit in the ear and imitate a hearing aid. He just had to get used to having something stuck in his ear. This was getting exciting, and at the very least he could see some movement in the case.

Vance was waiting for him in Starbucks.

"So you've arranged for a visit?"

"I haven't been to the beach for years even though I can see ours from my bedroom windows."

It was true. When he was not working, there were other things to do, and even going to their spectacular beach never was high on their list.

"How are you going to talk to Bradbury?"

"I don't have any particular plan. I know I'll ask him about the case, but from then on, well, I will probably let him talk. I have nothing to lose. The most important thing so far is that he agreed to see me. Obviously Tom has his own interest in the case. I'll try to find out what that is. Any legal advice from you?"

"I really don't know just what we'll do with any information we get from him. I just hope it's going to change the direction of this path we've been on. Good luck, Jack."

24

After a layover in Atlanta, Jack landed in Raleigh before eight. He ordered a bagel in the airport restaurant and went down to Hertz rentals where a car was waiting for him.

He took I-40 east, then from his car he called Tom.

"I will be waiting on the beach in front of the Blockade Runner Hotel. You can find me under a yellow umbrella. Oh, and when you come to the beach, wear shorts and a tank top. It's really sunny here." It sounded more like an order than friendly advice, Jack thought.

After a two-hour drive southeast to the port city of Wilmington, North Carolina, Jack was looking for his hotel in Wrightsville Beach. He had shorts, but went to a surf store to buy a tank top.

The day was sunny and the wind was down. Jack changed in the restroom at the hotel and left his belongings at the front desk. The beach was surprisingly quiet—not too many people were out. Jack saw the yellow umbrella to his left with a pier in the distance. Taking off his sandals, he started walking in that direction.

Tom Bradbury was sitting in a blue chair with an empty one next to him. He leaned back against the chair with his legs outstretched. He was looking much less timid than Jack remembered him from the operating room interactions. The tide was in, heavy waves falling white and noisy on the sand.

"Welcome to the other ocean, Dr. Murano. How was your flight?"

"Hello, Tom. And please call me 'Jack.' We are not in the operating room anymore. What are you doing in Wrightsville Beach?"

"Just taking a breather. As you probably know, my father is living in Chapel Hill and I help him around."

"How is he doing?"

"He is managing. Still working part time in the lab at the university, still trying to do his research. He and Mom have been divorced for quite a while. It didn't work out for them, either." Tom looked at the sand between his feet. "Did you have breakfast yet?"

"I did, kind of," Jack said.

More quiet.

Jack leaned over and started to explain why he had come here.

"Tom, you certainly know of the lawsuit Peter McCormick's family has filed against me. Have you read about this case? Do you remember it?"

"Do I remember!" Tom grinned. He nodded several times and gazed away toward the ocean.

Quiet came over them again.

"Do you know what happened to McCormick?"

"Sure I do. He ended up paralyzed." Bradbury was wiggling his toes and playing with sand. Then he looked straight at Jack. "Just like my father did."

Jack rested against the back of his chair, astounded. Just like that? Is he trying to tell me something? Was he really involved? Jack was becoming more and more suspicious.

"So how did it happen?"

"Since you got to me, you probably know at least that part of the story. And I'm sure you know about my father's accident."

Jack nodded, not wanting to interrupt.

"I was always close to my father. Closer than my sister. His career as a researcher always fascinated me, and I loved the quiet, unhurried life he had. Our bond was in sports. We started with baseball, but then I got interested in lacrosse. It became my favorite, and Father had always supported me. He had played basketball himself in college and saw team sports as the best way to help kids grow. He felt they developed discipline and strengthened our sense of commitment.

"I remember early-day practices and games, and long trips to away games with a lot of time to bond. In his car we talked and talked, and sometimes we didn't. I was planning game strategy and my dad was always listening. He didn't try to tell me what to do, didn't try to coach his own son. He was even known for carrying my equipment bag, though he knew well he wasn't supposed to. We always hoped that I would be accepted to Duke's stellar lacrosse program. The fact that my father graduated from there would be a plus, we thought.

"Besides sports we really enjoyed camping together. We have Jordan Lake here, and the camping spots are great. We both are quiet people, and the still, flat lake area was ideal for us."

Tom was looking away from Jack while talking, as if he didn't want Jack's facial expression to influence his story.

"After the accident everything changed. Dad spent close to two months in ICU and then three months in rehab. He was never been able to work as before.

"Then was the trial. I was there. What struck me was how cool and deliberate the proceedings were. Here is my father, barely able to sit in the wheelchair, and over there this bunch of guys trying dissect the minutiae of his accident. No compassion, no pity. And no remorse on McCormick's face. I was so angry, but I didn't know how to express it.

"We found out that the police didn't do a good job in collecting and preserving the evidence, and this soulless lawyer from Charlotte tore apart whatever evidence was left. We ended up with nothing. By the end of the trial, their lawyer came up with an offer and we did not appeal. I don't know how much money was involved, but Dad was able to buy a house in Fearrington."

"When did you decide to go to anesthesia school?"

"I always wanted to be a research fellow, like my dad. But then I realized I liked to work with people. Medical studies were my first choice, but I didn't have enough money. I still wanted to be at Duke, so CRNA school was my next choice. I really loved that school and I had the best teachers. Then it was time to start looking for a job."

Had Tom an agenda?

"So you were following McCormick."

"I found out where he was from my classmate who graduated a year ahead of me and had moved to California. Like McCormick did."

"You were planning everything carefully then?"

Tom went on.

"I couldn't get a job in your hospital. CRNAs were not allowed to work on the staff in the OR then. But with all the changes in health care and cost-cutting, they gave in and I was hired."

Two couples with noisy young children went by splashing and looking for seashells.

"I knew that sooner or later he was going to end up on the operating table. By that time I had enough seniority and I was making the OR assignments."

"So you put yourself on McCormick's case."

"Right."

"And you set up an epidural tray."

"Right."

"What did you draw into the syringe?"

"I had two choices. Either phenol or alcohol. Both in high concentrations cause extensive nerve damage. Alcohol smelled more natural in an OR environment. A smell of phenol would raise suspicion. So I drew 95 percent alcohol."

Jack looked at Bradbury, meeting his eyes straight on.

"That's a vicious plan!" No change in expression came to Tom's face. But Jack was astounded by how much planning, commitment, and perseverance he'd had to exert to attain such a cold-blooded goal.

"But what if we had decided not to do an epidural?"

"I would disable oxygen sensors on the anesthesia machine and temporarily turn off the oxygen flow," he said easily, still looking at Jack.

Jack gasped. Now he realized who he was up against. Tom's hatred was much greater and deeper than Jack had ever imagined. There was something unusual about it. One had to have a really good reason to go to this extent to decide to hurt another human being, then wait for twenty years to do it.

"Why are you telling me all this?"

"First of all, you asked me, Jack." Tom was quiet and his voice was calm. "And the second—you are really the only person I can talk to about it."

"Aren't you afraid I'll report what I've just heard?"

"Not really. No one would believe you. No proof exists, and you are just an interested party. I also asked you to come here dressed down as much as possible, so you could not wear a wire. In addition, the beach noise would be hard on any recording device, and besides it would not be admissible anyhow."

Jack regarded the waves. The beach had quieted, but a little boy was trying to surf regardless. His father was yelling instructions to him from the shore. The boy kept falling off the board, but each time he got up and tried again. His father was encouraging him and praising the effort.

Jack didn't have any more questions. The case seemed to come to a reasonable conclusion as far as the motive for this cold-blooded action against Peter and who did it. From the legal point, well, it was another story. The trial was still on. There were many things he needed to discuss with Vance.

Jack was thinking of the flight home. He had booked a return flight from RDU for tomorrow afternoon and had the morning free. He would drive to Chapel Hill and perhaps meet Tom Bradbury's father again. There was nothing keeping him here.

He got up and was ready to leave when Tom spoke.

"Jack, there is one more thing you should know about before you go. . . . Peter McCormick molested me when I was a boy."

25

Jack felt like he'd turned on a pair of noise-cancelling headphones. He turned back and sat down again in the beach chair. His head was spinning, and he leaned forward. Unaware of crashing waves or seabirds cawing above, Jack saw only Tom's head in a sort of tunnel vision.

"What the hell . . . ?"

"I knew you'd want to hear this story, too, Jack, but I have to go now. I can meet you in the restaurant on the pier, let's say . . . at seven? I'll be at a window table. Since you don't know the area, I'll even make the reservations. See you later," Tom said, walking off.

Jack remained seated for a few moments. Out of the blue all his problems had become insignificant and distant. He had a picture of a young boy in the hands of a predator. And the boy had Luke's face.

He rose and walked toward the hotel to check in despite feeling he was still in a fog.

From the lobby Jack called Diane, describing his conversation with Tom and leaving the fact of Tom's abuse for last.

She was as shocked as he had been.

"You have to talk with Vance, Jack. Besides the tragedy, it may be a game-changer for our trial."

Jack looked at his phone. It was after 9 a.m. in California, so Vance was probably in his office.

"Incredible!" was Vance's response after Jack finished explaining.

"Vance, I've recorded everything on my iPhone. The quality is not pristine, but the recording is understandable. He describes exactly his way of doing the crime. And then even having a plan B."

"I don't even want to know how you did it, Jack. It's not admissible under any circumstances. That's another reason why Tom was so open with you. And there is no factual support for whatever he said. Just your word and you are partial there. He knew that his story would not be admissible in a court of law."

"I realize that," Jack said, "but it helps me see the entire case better. And I can understand his motives. All this said, I am shocked how evil and premeditated this guy is to wait for such long time and accomplish his wicked and vengeful goal. Just wait, Vance, till you hear the rest of his story!"

Jack knew he needed some rest after the overnight flight and his eventful time at the beach.

The restaurant on the pier at Wrightsville Beach has a spectacular view of the ocean. The sun had moved to the west. *Probably right over California by now*, Jack thought. Tom was sitting at the corner table looking out to sea. Jack sat down and waited for his host to begin.

"My parents home-schooled us and then sent us to a small religious school," Tom started. "We are quiet people. We were proud of our heritage. They told me of our rejection of violence and war. Also to our opposition to slavery. Our ancestors apparently signed a document denouncing slavery by the end of the seventeenth century."

The waiter came to ask for orders, but they just ordered drinks for now.

"We had a very peaceful family life. I've never heard my parents arguing. All their problems were solved by a civilized discussion. Even when I did something wrong, there was never any real punishment. Just explanation and my promise never to do it again. We lived a simple life, very happy.

"In school we had to sit in silence for a half an hour each morning. That was time for our private conversation with God. Not everybody could do it, but I finally learned."

Throughout this, Jack looked at Tom steadily, wondering how a person with this kind of happy, peaceful upbringing could commit such an egregious and premeditated act.

"School was fun, but I really liked sports. Out of all the choices, lacrosse appealed to me the most. The quickness of the game captivated me! But the best of all was the teamwork, meaning you didn't have to have the best players to have a winning team. Average players with a good work ethic and a proper attitude, combined with competent, mature coaching, could put together an exceptional team. My father liked the idea of lacrosse because this skill would help me to get into Duke, he said."

When the waiter came again, it was time to order.

"In our second year of high school lacrosse, we got a new assistant coach," Tom said, "a young man from Duke. He played for their team and apparently was quite good. He liked my way of playing and saw my potential. Or so he said. During one of the practices, he showed me a few moves. One other time he pointed out another way to get around the defender. My skills were improving, which didn't go unnoticed by the head coach. My recognition on the team was getting better and better. Playing was fun and I felt the sense of accomplishment. . . . And the girls were noticing me, too.

"I grew up at home and in school with an atmosphere of respect for authority. The attention from the assistant coach, a successful Duke player, gave me a boost in my self-esteem. The fact that he saw a bright future for me in the game also gave me an incentive to practice even more. Getting recruited by Duke seemed closer and closer.

"It didn't take long for him to have meetings with me arranged outside team practice times and eventually in his home. It was his idea to make a videotape of an interview with me and include clips from my games. I would use the tape when I applied to colleges for an athletic scholarship. I was on a roll!

"And then on one of these 'taping sessions,' it happened. I will never forget the feelings I had after the encounter. It was like the world had just ended. I could never understand how I let him do it. He told me not to say anything about it to anybody. 'First, no one will believe you, and then your lacrosse career will be over. And you will never get into Duke,' Peter said.

"My lacrosse career didn't last past high school and I didn't get to Duke either. I ended up at UNC. But at least for the anesthesia school I was able to enroll at my father's alma mater. It's one of the best in the country." Tom finally found a reason to smile.

Jack tried to eat but realized he wasn't hungry. The sun was down, and the lights in the restaurant came on.

"And then my dad's accident happened. I was hit twice, since I soon realized that the guy who hit him was the same person who violated me while on the lacrosse team. I was boiling inside, but I didn't tell anyone. I didn't want to add to my father's misery. His life was shattered. And so were ours. My dark secret was eating me up.

"My father couldn't work to his potential anymore. Not being able to cope with all these events, he and Mom got divorced and our family fell apart."

The sun was gone, and all that was visible was the reflection of the restaurant lights on the waves. The waiter came again, but the pair sent him off.

"I watched the entire trial proceedings," Tom continued. "My dad was in his wheelchair, and Mr. McCormick didn't even look at him. If he realized who I was, and he must have, he didn't let it be known to me and probably to anybody else, for that matter. I didn't see any remorse on his face either. I hated him so much at this point, but I didn't wish him ill at that point. That changed, though, when the case was dismissed on technicalities. Appeared the police didn't do a good job. And his Charlotte lawyer seemed to be an arrogant, miserable human being.

"I was sincerely hoping for a hard punishment for him, but that hasn't happened. At that point I decided to deliver my own justice to Peter McCormick, even if would take me half of my life to wait for that moment.

"So they let him off. My father was not talking much. Mom moved to Charlotte and he got a house in Fearrington. Later on I got a message that McCormick had moved out of the area. And this was the end of it. Just like that.

"But not as far as I was concerned." Tom had fire in his eyes.

"I have a friend who is a private investigator and he, God only knows how, found out that Peter McCormick had moved to California."

"So you got the job in our hospital," Jack said, trying to speed up the conversation. He couldn't stand much more of this dismal yet heartbreaking downward-driven story.

"I actually applied to both, yours and the one in the next town. I didn't know which one he was using."

It was late and the food was cold. Jack heard waves crashing on the beach. The wind had picked up with the rising tide, and the woman on the beach held onto her elaborate hat as she walked in the face of the wind.

"Sorry, Jack, for piling all this on you," Tom said, looking pale. "You didn't do anything wrong. You are an excellent doctor, and all that time I truly enjoyed working with you. You've always handled yourself with class," he said, his voice dry and tired- sounding, then he glanced again at the dark, crashing sea.

Then he looked in Jack's eyes with sorrowful expression but without losing his decisiveness. "You are the first and the last person who will hear this story." He slowly nodded once, then another time and again, and then looked away at the angry sea. "Even my father doesn't know as much as you do. It would break his heart."

There was quiet at the table.

"Allow me to pay the bill," Tom reached for his wallet.

"Good-bye, Tom." Jack rose and walked away, feeling like a second, unwitting casualty of one-sided war between Tom Bradbury and Peter McCormick.

26

It was three hours earlier in California, so Jack still had time to call Diane. The motives in this case were clear now. It didn't change Jack's legal situation, though. The lawsuit was still on. He called Vance, but his friend was not available. His secretary promised that Vance would return Jack's phone call after work.

Jack's room was on the highest floor of the hotel, so he had a magnificent view of the super moon that night. That spectacular image was enhanced by a trail of light reflected on the broken, moving surface of water. It was an unforgettable scene.

Vance called when Jack was dressed in his pajamas and trying to watch the local news, though he wasn't following it at all.

"Are you still in the office? It's ten o'clock here."

"Yeah, I am. I have a deposition tomorrow. A litigation with a big company. How did the rest of your day go?"

It took a long time to relate the story Jack had learned that afternoon and evening.

"And he didn't tell anybody. Even his father doesn't know."

"How did you part with him?"

"He apologized and said he was sorry that all of it fell on me. He didn't sound, however, as though he regrets what *he's* done. He sacrificed a big chunk of his life to deliver his kind of justice." Tom still couldn't get over the scale of hatred and perseverance Jack displayed.

"Well, what's new for us, Vance?"

"It still doesn't look as if they found the expert witness to support their grievances. In view of that, I am thinking of filing a motion for a summary judgment to have the entire case dismissed. I think we have about a fifty-fifty chance."

"Don't hold your breath, Vance. Though I wish you the best of luck."

Jack walked over to the window. The moon was much higher now, and the view was different, more silvery yet still magnificent. And from the last floor in the hotel he had the perfect viewing point.

It was clear to him now how strong the bond was between Tom and his father. The sports events, the camping trips to Jordan Lake. Had he ever disciplined the boy? How was his balance between charging their emotional battery with good moments spent together and occasionally draining it with punishments? It must have been very strong, since it led Tom to such a crime of devotion. And he had never divulged his abuse at the hands of McCormick so as not to add to his father's misery following the accident.

Then Jack's mind shifted to his relationship with Luke. Was it strong enough to push him to commit such an extreme but still loyal act of revenge? He hoped Luke wouldn't ever be put in such a position, and if he were, perhaps he would never make such a stark choice. Perhaps he would learn to talk out his anger with the others involved.

Jack felt that his emotional bank with his son was full. He was working hard on it, trying to spend as much quality time with the boy as his busy schedule allowed him. Sometimes even more that that. Several times he'd been able to bend his operating-room and office time around his son's activities.

Then another strange thought came to him. He was thinking of his own funeral. People would gather to deliver eulogies. *What would Luke have to say about me? What is the ultimate measure of a father-son relationship? Does our relationship—Luke's and mine—come within hailing distance of that?*

Jack shook his head with rueful smile and went to bed.

27

Diane was waiting for Jack at LAX. She looked lovely in a flowing summer dress with sunflowers and silver and cream sandals as she gave him a hug. They both walked to baggage claim.

"How was your flight?"

"Long. Why do the westbound flights always take longer than the eastbound ones? Oh, never mind . . ." It really was a long trip, physically and emotionally. Diane knew the details of the conversations with Tom but didn't know Vance's plans.

"He doesn't think the other side has an expert witness yet. They may not be able to get anybody strong enough to support their side after all."

Diane drove easily through the heavy airport traffic.

"He is filing the motion for summary judgment. We have about a fifty-fifty chance, he says, for the judge to dismiss the case."

"It would be nice, also reasonable!" Diane was tired of the entire situation. Now, when they knew who did it and why, it was even more difficult to accept it, since not much could be done to prosecute.

The next day the three of them sat in Vance's office to discuss Jack's trip. He brought his iPhone and they all heard the recording loud and clear. The beach noise was mild at the beginning, then increased some by the end of the day. At dinner Jack didn't turn it on.

"It doesn't matter." Vance was implacable. "We can't use it anyhow."

"Can't we at least present it to the other side, to let them know there is an explanation for what happened?" Jack asked.

"And tell them the other part of the story? They won't listen to you. They will ask for proof and Bradbury will deny. What's worse,

Judy McCormick will find out about the molestation. So you tell me: Is it better to know or not to know it?" Vance was trying to present his argument.

"It is always better to know the truth," Diane was adamant. "And I would surely want to know if *my* husband was a stalker and predator of young boys!" "But sometimes it's better just to let it go. Think of Judy when she found out about it. Their marriage would be over," Vance was thinking as a lawyer.

But Diane leaned to the feminine view of the dilemma. "Let's assume we don't tell her and later on she somehow finds about her husband's transgression and Tom's monstrous plot. Is she going to blame Peter more for what he did to Tom or Tom more for what he did to Peter? Usually women stand by their husbands, but do we have the right to withhold this information and make that decision for her? She is the only one who could decide. And in the future, if somehow we become friendly again and she finds out the real story, will she ever forgive us? That would be an end to our relationship, I would think."

"Too many ifs. And I am still angry with them with their suit. The have co-opted and blighted a big part of our lives and there is no end in sight," Jack was determined. "Tom was right in thinking that the second part of this story would not go much further. He is done. As far as he is concerned, justice was served by revenge and he got what he wanted. I think our best move is to file a motion for a summary judgment."

All three agreed that that was the right decision to take now.

The surface of life seemed quiet, like the sea at low tide. The same office visits, the same cases in OR. The volume of Jack's patients, however smaller, had at least stopped falling. All the hoopla and drama generated by the trial seemed to have evaporated. Jack's partners still hadn't asked to renegotiate the reimbursement formula. At least not yet.

The motion for summary judgment was filed and a court date set.

28

In June time came for the Muranos' family vacation.

Spending time together during summer break was one of their earliest traditions, begun when the kids were very young and traveled within this country. In their Suburban they had covered most of the western United States. Later on, when the kids grew older and had seen most of the places within reach by car, it was time to go abroad. Jack and Diane met in a Club Med resort and liked its convenience and relaxed style, so it seemed a good fit for their family, too.

Tahiti was their destination for this year. The parents liked the authenticity and pristine climate of the island, and the kids . . . well, they'd love it, too, after they saw it.

For Jack it was another opportunity to be with twelve-year-old Luke as the boy was growing up. It was interesting to see him interact with his friends, his older sister, and other adults. Jack tried not to be too strict in correcting Luke's actions but rather guide him by example.

He tried to compare Luke's experiences with those of his own childhood. Remembering that his own father hadn't given Jack too much attention while he was growing up, Jack wanted to make sure Luke got enough of the right kind now.

Luke's seat in the plane was next to Jack's. He was wearing headphones, drowning in music only he could understand. Jack looked at his son. How he'd grown in the past two years! A few years ago the boy had problems with asthma, and at times Jack and Diane were very worried about him. During soccer and hockey games his inhaler gave only temporary relief.

For one of their trips east with Luke's school, Jack took a week off to be a chaperone for the group and to help teachers manage this large bunch of sometimes unruly kids. The trip was during winter and the weather was severe. Sightseeing at the nation's capital was unforgettable, full of memories meant to last a lifetime.

However, by the end of their stay in DC Luke got sick. He had a fever and was having difficulty breathing. He became much worse on the flight back home to California. The boy was breathing heavily, and his coughing was difficult to control. He probably had pneumonia, and at such a high altitude, all this became worse. Jack had used every available over-the-counter remedy, but Luke showed no visible improvement. The boy was becoming restless and his face was gray. Jack was panicking. *I have to tell the pilot to land the plane and get Luke some real help!* he thought. They moved to the back of the plane and Jack used newspaper to fan the air around the boy's face. It helped a bit and soon they landed at LAX. While on the ground the boy felt better and Diane took over and nursed him to some stability. The next day his pediatrician did the rest.

When Jack described what had happened on the plane and how scared he was, Diane looked at him and said, "Why didn't you ask the pilot to drop you one of these oxygen masks from the ceiling of his plane? It would have helped!"

"Why didn't I? I just didn't think about it at that time. That's why doctors should never treat their families," Jack said, rediscovering a common truth.

Later on Luke grew out of his asthma. With no more dramatic breathing crises, Luke could exercise freely.

Now Luke was sitting next to him, listening to his music and looking out over the Pacific absentmindedly.

Ever since Luke started to walk, Jack tried to sense what he was going to be good at. As his own father had done for Jack, Luke was exposed to sports and music. What would Luke like the best? He liked sports activities, and now probably was a good time to introduce him to music. Jack played both classical and popular music stations while on the long car trips. The next step was to see if he would like to play in a school band. The boy would make his own choices, Jack knew. It would be interesting if Luke liked both, because Jack did.

However, being a professional musician or an athlete was not what Jack had in mind. His goal in having Luke practice music and sports was for his son to know and appreciate different aspects of life better—and to widen his horizons. It was not Jack's idea to push him in any specific direction, certainly not to say or even imply that he expected him to become a doctor, or a musician. Just present him different possibilities from which he could choose.

He remembered a few of his friends who were sent to schools of their parents' choice. The parents would pay only for the school they chose. That tactic commonly would end up in a loss of time and money, and a huge damage to the parent-child relationship, sometimes even in tragedy.

Jack's father was a lawyer, and Jack remembered conversations with him before the deadline to choose a college.

"Dad," Jack said, "you are a very successful lawyer and I know you want me to follow in your footsteps. But I dream of being a doctor and want to apply to medical school. I think I'll do better in medicine than in law."

"Jack, that's just great," his father answered. "I've always wanted to be a doctor, but I couldn't get to medical school." That settled his problem. He had the full support of his father after that honest conversation.

The flight attendant offered snacks, and Luke chose orange juice and peanuts. Nothing original here, Jack was thinking while watching Luke change the program on his iPhone.

The hockey adventure had required a lot of commitment from both of them.

One Friday Jack had the full OR schedule. Later on he went to see the patients in his office. Then was a time for dinner. Since he was on duty that weekend, late at night he received a call from the ER.

A patient with a stab wound to his chest had just been brought in after an altercation with his friends. He didn't look that bad but had to be taken to the operating room and the bleeding had to be stopped. He started surgery at midnight, and after three o'clock Jack was closing the patient's chest. His anesthesiologist looked at him and said, "It will be so good to go home, won't it? Have a nice breakfast, a warm shower, and sleep till noon?"

"I hope you will," Jack said. "We have a hockey practice at six with

Luke, so I will just have time to shower, change, maybe eat something, and then go. We have to be at the rink an hour before the practice."

The anesthesiologist looked at Jack, startled. "If I had to do all that for my son, he wouldn't play hockey." He was a recently married young man with no children on his own. *That will change when you have a son,* Jack thought, smiling to himself.

Playing ice hockey in California was certainly an unusual activity in 1990. It was barely two years after the Gretzky trade and all the hoopla was just beginning. Rinks were still sparse, though, and travel times to them were long. Some of their friends shook their heads in disbelief when Luke, with Jack's support, chose that sport.

And there was a misconception about hockey rife among their friends. They saw hockey players as a bunch of fighting goons with their front teeth missing. Jack saw hockey instead as a demanding sport where discipline and commitment count the most, coordination and physical fitness are paramount, and proper rapport with teammates decides whether you have a winning team. For Jack it was the essence of all successes in life.

And above all, the Muranos plainly enjoyed hockey.

The plane landed in Papeete and a ferry took them to the resort. After checking in, changing into their beach clothes, and looking around, Luke said, "It looks like Hawaii!" They'd been there before, a year ago, on the previous family outing. Jack smiled, "Kind of, but not the same. These islands are more natural and less crowded. You'll see the difference by the time we leave to go home."

On the beach Luke saw another difference right away, but he didn't mention it until the third or fourth day of their stay.

"Dad, women look different here." Club Med was filled with young women who conformed to more relaxed, European beach customs.

"That's true," Jack said.

"Mom doesn't dress like that."

"Right, she doesn't."

"Why?" Luke was prodding.

Jack thought for a moment.

"Do you play cards, Luke?"

"Sure, I do. With my friends."

"Do you play poker?"

"I don't, Paul does." Paul was their next-door neighbor, mature beyond his age.

"I don't play much, either," Jack explained. "But there are a few rules I know. One of them is that you don't show your cards to people you play with. At least at the beginning of the game. You do it later. And only to people of your choice, so you can have control of your game."

Luke looked at Jack. "What do you mean, Dad?"

After a few seconds his face brightened with a sly smile.

"I get it, Dad! Mom's taking more care and control of her body than those women. That's good, right?" "Yes, Luke, it really is. For her and for you and me, too."

Good for him. If doesn't get it fully now, I hope he understands in a few years, Jack thought.

The rest of the vacation kept them light years away from California.

29

The Polynesian vacation came to an end when their plane landed at LAX and Jack turned his phone on again. They'd lived in a partially true, partially self-imposed blackout from the real world while they were in Tahiti. While on the island at first Jack had the strange sense that something was missing when he received no messages from the office and from the hospital. But in a few days he got used to free-flowing time and even came to like the lack of interruptions. Soon he lost all the feeling of guilt, and he was enjoying his temporary freedom immensely. *Is this how retirement will feel?* he wondered often. But that was out beyond the horizon, anticipated but not welcomed yet.

His phone was buzzing now, though, and messages started popping off. Email, email, another email, a few new Facebook messages, and then a text message from Vance. Jack stopped for a second. He had completely forgotten that the day before was Vance's court appearance on their motion for a summary judgment. "Call me as soon as you get this message," it read.

While their plane was taxiing to the gate, Diane was telling the kids to gather their belongings. Jack found Vance's number on his favorites list, and the lawyer picked up almost immediately.

"I had a good day in court yesterday, Jack. Judge Correy threw the case out. The only expert witness they could come up with wasn't even a cardiac surgeon. Some kind of a hired gun. I checked on him. He often testifies on behalf of anybody who pays his fees. Really pathetic."

Jack didn't hear the rest of the story.

"Vance, it sounds great! Excellent job. But I just landed at LAX. Can I call you later?"

"Sure. I will be in the office all day tomorrow."

Diane looked at him concerned.

"What's wrong? Something happen?"

"Yes. Vance was in court yesterday with our motion for summary judgment. The judge threw the case out!"

"Should I believe it?" Diane asked as the jet engines wound down and then shut off. Jack could see tears in her eyes. "Is it final? No more legal wrangling, just like that?"

"I am not sure about the details, but Vance sounded ecstatic. I will call him tomorrow."

They were both so tired that they even didn't want to think of possible consequences. Tomorrow will be another day.

The next day Jack called Vance between two cases in the OR. First, Vance described the procedure at the hearing. The other side was betting on the terrible injury that Peter McCormick had suffered while under Dr. Murano's care, followed by the loss of his health and earning power. Vance on the other side argued that Dr. Murano had nothing to do with it. In view of weak support from the plaintiff's expert witness, the judge dismissed the case.

"The bad thing is that they still may sue your anesthesiologist," Vance said.

"But is my verdict final?" Jack couldn't take in the finality of the decision yet.

"Looks like that's all." Vance didn't want to commit himself for sure. "I'll send you the final decision when I get it."

"Thanks, Vance, for all your work. It'll take Diane and me quite a while for all this to sink in."

Dinner at home was quiet. After the kids went to their rooms to do their homework, it was time to decide what to do next. Even so, they remained at the table somewhat listlessly, not knowing how and where to start. The war was over, and it was time to start rebuilding the damage done to Jack's practice, their relationships, and their finances, but what about their reputation? That was a huge yet ineffable problem, thus hard either to gauge or to mend.

Would the local paper publish news of the suit's dismissal? Probably not. But if so, it would be water under the bridge. The damage had already been done. The Muranos had lost some of their friends over something having nothing to do with them, and this loss probably hurt the most. They were glad, of course, to know the truth as Tom told it, but even so, Jack and Diane knew it would be a long way back to normalcy.

For one thing Jack couldn't get over McCormick's horrible complication. It had sunk deeply into Jack's psych, like stage fright. Each time he stepped into the operating room, he thought of all the possible things that could happen to his patient. During surgery it wasn't as bad, but after that it was a nightmare until the patient was discharged home. And even then, so many things could happen to him, and the worst eventualities kept coming to Jack's mind, haunting him even for weeks after each surgery. It was extremely hard for Jack to relinquish this self-defeating pattern of worry.

30

After dinner one evening the next week, Diane was talking on the phone to her mother, who was concerned that Diane's father was not doing well. Both parents were in their eighties and used to travel to see Jack, Diane, and the grandkids frequently. Recently, however, their stamina just wasn't there, but their phone calls were becoming more frequent.

The phone on the business line rang, and the operator from the answering service said, "They need you in ER. Can I put them through?"

"It's OK. I'll call them myself," Jack said, not wanting to tie up the line in case of a longer conversation. He dialed the emergency department number.

"Dr. Murano speaking. Are you guys looking for me there?" Jack could hear a noisy background with everyone talking at the same time over sirens and the beeps of heart monitors.

"Dr. Kantor wants to talk to you." Ed Kantor was one of the older and more experienced physicians there and a close friend of Jack's. They came to the community together and used to see each other socially often. Now, with all the changes in healthcare and the many new and younger doctors on the hospital staff, it was more business and fewer birthdays, celebrations, and traditional Christmas parties. Then again, their kids were older, and there were fewer opportunities to meet over soccer games or swim meets.

"Hey, Jack, thanks for calling back." Ed had been busy and Jack had had to wait for him to pick up the phone. "I have a problem here. We've got a car accident with three people involved. One is dead on the scene, no seat belts. Another one, from the backseat, has only minor injuries. The driver is alive and stable, but has a wide mediastinum on the chest X-ray, and may have aortic dissection. He's been drinking. Oh, and one more thing. His last name is McCormick. He may be Peter's son."

Jack's jaw dropped. Suddenly nothing else mattered. *God, why me again?* he thought.

Diane was still on the phone. "I need to go to the ER." He didn't tell her the whole story. "I may be back late."

While in his car on the way to the hospital, Jack thought of the young man in the ER. What if he *is* Peter's son? He was alive, but that type of injury, if confirmed, could be devastating. One of the complications of surgery for traumatic aortic dissection, Jack was perfectly aware, was paraplegia. The boy could end up in a wheelchair just like his father. *Will Judy even let me operate on her son? Or should I recuse myself from doing this surgery if it comes to that? Or should I just transfer him to another hospital?*

Jack knew that in a true emergency, like this, transfer to another hospital was out of question. His partners were on vacation, so no one else was available. *It's either me or no surgery at all if she won't consent. Could the boy be treated in ICU without surgery, at least initially? Well, yes, it's theoretically possible, but the risks are high and the chances for severe complications are prohibitive. I am not ready for that—but are the risks worse than suffering through this surgery on my own?*

The ER was busy as always. Jack parked in a designated spot and a familiar security guard let him in. The young man was still in the CT suite with a nurse. Jack looked through the chart that for some reason was still at the front desk. Yes, it was him, Steven. Same first name and the age was right. He went to the same school as Jack's children. His vitals looked good, no signs of decompensation, no signs of massive internal bleeding.

"Any other injuries? Head trauma?"

"Nothing we found so far." Ed was looking at the computer screen. "Just a terrible blunt chest trauma, despite seat belts and an air bag. He hit a parked eighteen-wheeler."

Jack went to the CT scanner suite and saw the boy on the ventilator, sedated. Then he talked to the tech. "Who is the one reading tonight?"

"We have nighthawk services tonight, Dr. Murano." Nighthawk services were provided by a radiologist in another time zone, sometimes in another country, who would read and interpret CT images from the computer screen.

Jack hated that. Nothing beats face-to-face communication. He always wondered how the hospital medical staff office solves the problems of granting privileges and obtaining medical malpractice coverage for doctors half a world away. He shook his head, having to take what was given tonight.

After the technician reconstructed all the images, Jack looked through them himself. There was no doubt that young Steven McCormick had an aortic dissection. He saw a tear in the aorta in a typical place, right after it gave up the branch to the left arm. No signs, though, of any significant internal bleeding. He had then some time and didn't have to rush the boy straight to the operating room, but surgery had to be done within the next few hours.

Because the boy had multiple rib fractures, he was intubated and sedated so as not to fight the ventilator. Jack went back to the ER. "The patient's mother is waiting for you in a conference room," one of the nurses said, showing him the way.

"Hi, Judy." She was sitting there, again with her sister. The waiting room was small and quiet despite all the surrounding ruckus. Again, she sat in the edge of her chair, tilted forward with both hands on her knees.

"Hi, Jack. How is he?"

"He is stable. Had a bad blunt chest trauma. Quite a few rib fractures. They put him on the ventilator and he is sedated."

"Can I see him?" Judy interrupted.

"No, not now. He's still in X-ray." Jack hesitated. "But that's not all."

Judy turned her head sharply and furrowed her forehead. "What?"

"Judy, your son has an aortic dissection." Jack was watching her face carefully.

"What is that?"

"The blunt trauma was so powerful that it partially tore his aorta."

"What does that mean? Can you fix it?"

"Yes, I can. But it also means that if we do not operate on the tear or are not successful, he may end up paralyzed from the waist down."

Judy's shoulders fell and her energy dissipated before his eyes. She looked deflated, started shaking, and didn't seem to be aware of Jack or her sister.

"Again?" she said to no one in particular. The room was quiet, though Jack could hear muffled noises outside and sirens from the ER communication room with the police scanner on. Judy leaned even more forward and covered her face with both hands. It was another minute before she spoke.

"Do I have any other choices?"

"You do, but not good ones," Jack was trying to speak as gently as possible.

"I have to call Peter. Unfortunately he is on the East Coast."

"Sure," Jack said. "And I have to call the OR, call the anesthesiologist and also reschedule my operations for this morning. Just in case."

He left the small waiting room and walked toward the OR.

In the surgeons' lounge the coffee was hot but thick and bitter, at least twelve hours old.

31

Jack was the only surgeon qualified and be available to do this case. But should he do it?

What about treating young Steven in ICU till the next morning and then transferring him to University Hospital? Yet if his aorta was to rupture, which could happen at any time, and massive bleeding ensue, the boy would die and this would be an end for Jack, too. No further defensive action could be taken for him. So Jack would have to operate as soon as logically possible without just rushing the boy straight to the operating room. The timing of the surgery was precarious. On top of that, the emotional pressure was enormous for him; it was like operating on a member of his own family—except that his family would never sue after a bad outcome. Jack had gone through hell in living with the fiasco of McCormick's litigation. Only recently had he been able to sleep a little better. And now this had happened.

He called the anesthesiologist on call for tonight.

"Did they sign the consent?" was Rick's only question, his voice muffled and raspy.

"Not yet, they are still thinking."

"Call me when they do," Rick said and hung up.

This was a typical, played-out routine.

— *Why do you wake me up when you are not sure about me being needed there?*

— *I want to give you heads up.*

— *I don't need your heads up in the middle of the night. I can be there in fifteen minutes anyhow.*

That was the predictable conversation the next day. Jack should have known better.

The pump technician was on his way. The OR nursing crew was in the lounge, but Jack knew it would take at least another hour to set the room up.

Surprisingly, Jack liked doing surgery in the middle of the night. It was quiet, and no phone calls interrupted his work. He liked having the OR just to himself, but not in emotionally loaded cases like this one. He hoped that he would settle down once the incision was made. After that it would be just a routine procedure. But what about Judy? And Peter? All this waiting would be a nightmare for them.

He went back to the conference room to talk to the boy's mother again. The ER noise was toned down. Judy was sitting at the edge of her chair, motionless, looking at the floor, her sister next to her.

"Did you have a chance to talk to Peter?"

Judy straightened up. "I just spoke with him." She was calm and composed, her eyes wide open, though teary, and locked on Jack. She sounded determined, her voice low and decisive.

"We both would like you to operate on our son," she said slowly, unmoving, then paused.

"And may God bless you," she added looking up at Jack.

Another pause.

"Both of you."

Jack nodded his head, bent over, hugged her, and left the room. He went to the OR to change. It was quiet, and he recalled Gary Cooper getting ready for the gunfight in *High Noon.*

32

Doing complex surgery is a lonely proposition, Jack thought. It's you and the elements, not just you and the patient. Plenty of things have to go right for a patient to come home without any complications. Many personal and technical factors are in play before a procedure can claim success. An entire operating team, anesthesia team, pharmacist, and all the support people in the OR have to be on alert and work in synch. Innumerable technical maneuvers must be done exactly right and in a proper time. Correct doses of proper medications must be given at the appropriate moments. The complex machines and devices need to perform faultlessly. And on top of it, the surgeon has to make sure that everybody and everything is prompt and working well together. He is the "captain of the ship," and it's his job alone to guide them through high, often rough seas.

Many times he gets all the glory for good results, but sometimes the adulation is not fully deserved. He also often is blamed for poor results not always his fault. It comes with the task and territory. And no one asks him or cares whether he has personal problems on his mind. Well, Jack smiled to himself, a few patients did ask him before surgery if he slept well the night before or tried to take other soundings of his mood by framing awkward personal questions. In most cases, they make half-humorous small talk to signal him that they are not afraid at all, so he took their joking and small talk as a sign of confidence.

But whenever Jack heard people describing complications that occurred during the surgical procedures, he was always amazed that these mistakes didn't happen more often.

In changing to scrubs, only the pump tech was in the dressing room with him, but he left shortly to put the equipment together. Now Jack was alone with his quiet moment. Technically he knew what to do. Repairing an aortic tear was not a simple, everyday procedure; it happened only once or twice a year in this community. But he was comfortable in doing that operation. The crew was experienced and had worked together for years. Anesthesia was paramount, and Rick was working tonight or this morning. Jack had lost his sense of time passing.

What was unusual today was the heavy emotional baggage Jack was bringing to the operating room. The case of Steven's father's lawsuit had taken an enormous toll on Jack's personal and professional life. He had almost lost his practice, and for a while he felt he was being ostracized.

As of last week's decision, though, he felt vindicated, but his life was still out of balance. And it might never come back to normal. That remained to be seen. With still so much unsettled, could he go through with the surgery? Jack knew technically he'd be able to do it, but that was only a part of it; a skillful ship's captain without the sea legs who takes to his cabin in a tempest is, in effect, not a viable captain of the ship at all.

He prayed for a moment to have the mental fortitude to complete the surgery and for nothing unexpected to happen. It was between him and the boy now, and Jack wished him well. Jack realized then, oddly, that he could never be a pediatric surgeon since he felt that children should never be sick. "Peter's son is still just a boy," Jack said aloud, and flame rose in his chest.

"We are ready for you in the room," the voice on the intercom said, bringing him back to reality.

"I am coming."

"And here we go," Jack told himself softly as he walked to the sink and turned the water on.

In the waiting room Judy was sitting motionless next to her sister. Her head was tilted back, and her hands were restless. Every few minutes she got up, walked a few steps, and then sat down again. The small waiting room area seemed especially like a prison that day.

"When will Peter be coming home?" Sarah said.

"He is flying back very early in the morning. It was the first available connection. It takes four hours to get here and then his handicapped van will take him straight to the hospital. I hope they will be done by then."

Again the two were quiet, Judy staring at the wall. The noise outside subsided and it felt awkward. Judy stretched her legs out and
then put them under the chair again. Her head was resting on both
hands folded one on top of other.

"Judy, how do you feel about all this?" Sarah said.

"All I know my son is gravely sick."

Quiet again. The outside speaker announced the arrival of an
ambulance in two minutes. "But I am petrified, Sarah. Out of my
mind."

"Did we do the right thing?"

"What do you mean?" Judy turned to her sister.

"To let him operate on Steven?"

"I've been thinking of that all morning. After what happened between us I wouldn't let him touch my son. But then I called Peter. You
were here. He was much less emotional and he convinced me. After
we detach ourselves personally from him, Peter said, Jack is quite a
capable surgeon, and I'm sure will do a good job. Peter knows he
would not intentionally hurt Steven. And after all, we have no choice.
There is no other surgeon available, and transport was impossible. In
the end it was actually an easy decision."

"But now everything is in Jack's hands."

"Yep, and we all will have to live with the results."

The ambulance arrived at the ER and the sudden increase in activity and voices signified it was likely another multiple trauma patient. After a knock, a nurse opened the door and the noise from
outside intensified.

"Anything I can do for you? Coffee?" Judy was staring at the door.

"That would be nice," Sarah answered for both of them.

The door closed. Quiet again.

"Do you think they've started yet?" Judy asked.

"Probably not yet, Judy. When we met the anesthesiologist, he said
it takes a long time to get the equipment ready, the heart pump and
all, and only then they put him to sleep."

"Will he live? And if so, will he end up paralyzed?" This was the
question most deeply imbedded in Judy's mind.

Sarah didn't have an answer. No answer could change Judy's feeling of despair while she was waiting for the end of the surgery.

Outside the waiting room, activity was relentless. "Is the X-ray ready?" a nearby female voice asked, piercing the background noise in ER. "Tell them we're coming!" They heard more talk in the hall just outside the door, and then a child crying.

"Judy, lightning doesn't strike twice," was all Sarah could come up with.

"I'll let you know if you are right after the surgery is over. But keep your eyes on the skies and your ears primed for thunder in all this noise and chaos.

"I wasn't as terrified seventeen years ago before and during Steven's delivery. That seems so easy now." Judy started pacing in the tiny conference room, and again she sat down, looking as if she felt cornered, a tigress in a cage.

"I hope by now they've started."

The flash of noise from the ER hit their waiting room again. The nurse came in, bringing two cups of coffee. When she closed the door, silence returned.

"Sarah, do you think Jack can do a good job—and will want to—considering what has happened between us lately?"

"I have no doubts. He is an excellent surgeon," her sister answered.

"I know he is, Sarah. But do you think he will do everything in his power, going overboard if necessary to save my son?"

"He is a professional. I doubt he has much time to think about what happened back then. Or at least much time, while he's working over our Steven on the operating table. Judy, let's pray for both Steven and Jack. There is really no other way."

With that, they bowed their heads.

33

It was calm in the OR. No one talked. All knew Jack liked it that way during longer, more complicated cases. The monotonous hum of the ventilator played under the muffled ticking of the EKG monitor.

It was so quiet, Jack could hear himself think. He liked working in the middle of the night.

The first part was just routine, mechanical work of preparation for the main act: repair of the aorta. Jack felt great, without pressure from the past months' worries. It was just another problem to solve, though bigger than usual. Jack again was in a problem-solving mode. Maybe it required more creativity and people skills than, say, auto mechanics. And more and deeper knowledge. Still, it was a problem-fixing job, a lot like car repair.

They probably wonder if my hands are shaking, he smiled. *They never do, except when I drink too much coffee. I wonder what will happen when I get older?* One old surgeon had told him that handshaking was not a problem. The loss of stamina was. It was more difficult to get up in the middle of the night to go to the ER or answer calls from the ICU after being awakened. Also the recovery after a sleepless night took longer. How it would work out for him in twenty years? Could he keep up this grueling pace for that long? The kids would be out of college, probably on their own, and there would be less motivation to work that hard. He was also told by the older surgeons that a main concern for them was their own health problems. Jack didn't smoke and exercised fairly often, but you never knew. He didn't think much about his age, but he knew this might become a factor. Eventually.

He hoped he would know when to get out. He had seen so many older surgeons still around the operating room when their skills were gone and so were their patients. It was hard to watch.

"Ready for heparin?" he heard from behind the anesthesia screen.

"Give me a few minutes." The patient had to have a blood thinner to be connected to the pump machine. So far everything was going smoothly and the team was doing its job as expected.

"OK, let's heparinize now."

In the ER conference room the two women were trying not to show the pressure that was settling on them. Judy played solitaire on her phone. She often did it to relax, but it didn't help her today. Sarah was thinking of ways to keep her sister's mind off young Steven's surgery, but nothing was working. Judy's hands were trembling and her eyes were welling. "I don't know how much longer I can take it," she told Sarah.

"Jack said it may take three to four hours before they can tell you how they are doing," Sarah reminded her.

"Let's go on the pump."

"Here we go," Ron said, removing clamps from the tubes and turning the machine on.

The rollers started rotating, the drains turned red, the patient's blood pressure dropped. The preparations were over, and Jack had time to concentrate on the main part of the procedure to repair young Mc-Cormick's aortic tear. His concentration was complete and absent any room for thinking of personal problems—no Peter's fiasco in North Carolina, no lawsuit, and no Judy waiting in the ER conference room.

Jack was a music lover, and for him doing surgery sometimes resembled directing a symphony orchestra. As in a classical composition, sonata allegro, there was a first part, faster, followed by a second, slower, and third, often quite fast and then ending with resolution in form of finale or coda. If everything went well, he felt like taking a bow and saying "Thank you" to the operating team. Often Jack almost heard the applause.

He was deep in the second part of the surgery now—slow and deliberate movement with slight echoes of the first part worked in.

Jack didn't even notice music from behind the anesthesia screen softly playing arias from his favorite Italian operas.

34

Peter's flight was on time. He had come to the airport earlier than most since his departure took longer with his wheelchair accommodations. He asked for and received a seat with extra leg room. With several hours of flying ahead of him, Peter's sense of helplessness and not being in control were the worst, but he knew he just had to wait and try to be patient.

How was his and Judy's recent lawsuit against Jack going to affect his delivering the boy's care? Will he do the best job? He knew of this surgeon's integrity, though—that could be counted upon. And doctors do take an oath to do no harm. But no one knows. If something does happen, no one would be able to prove anything. And paralysis is a well-known complication, which happens even to the best of surgeons. *Look at what happened to me! And could Jack subconsciously do something to harm my boy?*

Peter didn't even notice a flight attendant asking him, "Coffee? Peanuts?"

He had put on a pair of noise-cancelling headphones to seal himself off.

"How is Judy?" he texted Sarah after she sent him a message saying that they hadn't started the surgery yet. *She must be worrying sick*, he thought.

Could Steven die? He certainly could. There was always that possibility. Could he be left paralyzed? This would be even worse. *He would be with us at home for the rest of our lives. I can't imagine two wheelchair-bound people in the same household! I'm going insane*, he decided. *Nothing like that is going to happen. The chances are minuscule. Not with the level of today's medical care. And Jack is a really good surgeon, plus he knows he is being watched.*

But if a slip-up does happen? *Oh, God, I don't even want to think about it! We'll know in a few hours. I wish I could be there with Judy now. It'll take some time to get from the airport to the hospital despite my van waiting for me there.*

The aortic repair was done. Jack checked for bleeding through the suture line. Leakage was minimal, and some was expected. It was time to reassess the results of his surgery realistically. While on the bypass Steven's blood pressure was low. Now it was time to get off the bypass, raise the blood pressure, and then let the heart support the entire body. Jack didn't expect many problems. The boy's heart was young, and the pump's running time was not very long.

"Can we come off?" Jack asked.

"Ready when you are," Ron said, waiting for the command.

Jack was watching Steven's young heart taking over. He had seen it happen so many times in his career, but each time he was in awe of it. When he was still in training and saw this part of open-heart surgery—as the deflated heart muscle slowly comes back to life—it always brought him childlike joy. The heart, which was stopped and quietly resting for an hour or so, gradually revives and starts beating again. In the meantime, by some definition the patient was dead, relying on machines to keep him alive. Then later the heart comes back to life, rejoining the rest of the body, like nothing had happened. For Jack, modern surgery was still mostly miracle.

He waited to see how stable the patient was. Everything seemed to look good.

He waited a little longer, watching the operating field. There was no bleeding, and the boy's heart was working well. He was ready to close.

"We are done here. Let's hear the closing music." Dan Fogelberg's voice filled the background, this time in rhythm with the EKG monitor beeps. Jack was vaguely amused by that, seeing the consonance as a good omen.

He allowed his mind to wander. Did Dan die first or did his father? He thought it was his father. It would be an unbearable pain for any father to bury his own son. No one should be put through that. It happened to a couple of his friends, and Jack couldn't watch them at the funerals. Both men are still not the same.

"Let's let the family know that we are closing and I will be talking with them shortly." The nurse picked up the phone to relay the message.

35

Judy was on her third cup of coffee. The ER was slow now, with only minimal noise outside the waiting room, but she didn't pay much attention. The nurse from the OR called a few minutes before to say that Dr. Murano would be there shortly. Apparently surgery had gone well and there was nothing unexpected. "He should be there soon," she said. The nurse sounded relaxed despite the early hours, her voice calm and reassuring.

"I wonder when Peter will be here. I want so much to have him with me," Judy said, walking back and forth again in a small room.

After a slight knock at the door, Jack came in. He looked tired, his surgical cap still on. Judy sat and froze in expectation, with her legs under the chair and hands on her knees.

"How did it go? How is he?"

"I have good news for you. Everything went smoothly, as expected. No complications."

Judy slumped in her chair, seemingly relieved and certainly unglued, ready to cry.

"He got a good repair and had no surprises. But he's not awake yet and we don't know anything about his legs. It may take a few hours."

"Can I see him now?" Judy jumped up.

"Well, not yet, he is still in the OR. You can see him in ICU in a few hours. He may be still on the ventilator and probably sedated. We'll let you know of any changes in his status." Judy seemed to be somewhat relieved, though she still had to wait for a final verdict.

"Oh, God, how I wish Peter was here with me!"

Peter's plane had just landed. He texted Judy as soon as the wheels touched the ground.

"Have they finished yet?"

"Yes, Peter! Jack came out and said it went OK, but Steven is not awake yet."

"When will they know?"

"In an hour or so. When will you be there?"

"About the same time."

"Come straight to the hospital. We are in the ICU waiting room."

"See you soon."

His van was ready and Peter slowly eased into the heavy LA traffic. His mind was running wild. So Steven had survived surgery, but it's not over yet. He couldn't imagine two wheelchairs in his home. He could get used to this, being older himself, but what about Steven? What a potential waste of a young life it could come to!

Traffic was lighter outside the city.

He would have a chance to have a good career behind the computer, or on the phone. But no sports. And travel would be more difficult. He could get married, but could he have children? I should probably accept that he is alive and not ask for anything more, Peter thought, trying to manage his expectations. *Just to have him around will mean the world to me.*

He knew, though, how tough it was to adapt to being unable to walk. Days seemed shorter, since preparations to do anything took significant amounts of time. And, despite all the modern accommodations, there was still no comparison to the access an able-bodied person had everywhere.

In the distance he saw the silhouette of the hospital.

So many bad memories! Bad results from the surgery, months spent in rehab. Then the remodeling of his house and his lengthy adjustment to a new lifestyle. Many dreams had been shattered, though some new avenues were opened. The good thing was they were financially taken care of. The bad? Well, he didn't want to think about it. And now it was Steven's accident, and he might have to relive all his bad experiences once again with his son.

The elevator in the hospital was spacious. They make them big enough to accommodate a full-size critical-care bed and all the necessary equipment, Peter realized.

He was familiar with the labyrinthine way to the ICU waiting room. He found Judy in a smaller room, which gave them more privacy. She and her sister were sitting in complete silence.

Peter wheeled in and hugged both women. He didn't have to ask the news. They both looked like campers after a night in the wilderness.

"Nothing yet?"

"Still not awake. Vitals are stable, though."

A few long minutes passed in complete silence among them in the room.

Then a soft knock roused the three. Noise from the main waiting room hit the closed space, and Peter saw Jack standing at the door, towering above him.

36

"Hi, Peter." Everyone was staring at Jack, Judy with eyes wide open. At this point she appeared ready to receive any news, good or bad.

Pause.

"The news is good," Jack said. "Steven woke up and is moving his legs. He is still on the vent, though."

Another pause, this time longer. Judy bent over and put her head in her hands and started to shake.

Is she laughing? Jack wondered. She began sobbing. Peter put his arm around her.

"Can we see him?" he asked Jack.

"Sure, I will show you to his room."

Peter was wheeling first, and his wife could barely keep up that pace. Jack opened the door of the boy's spacious ICU room. He let them in and then closed the door in front of himself. He had previously asked the nurse to leave and give McCormick enough privacy. Jack stayed outside and was watching through the huge glass door a scene from a silent movie.

Judy bent over and said something to her son. He raised his hand and touched his mother. She said something else and Jack saw first the right knee and then the left one lifted above the mattress. She gave him a bigger hug. Then she turned around and Jack saw tears in her eyes.

"Thank you," he read on her slowly moving lips.

Jack bowed his head slightly and moved his right hand toward his head in a gesture of salute. He felt a lump in his throat. Then he left McCormicks to celebrate in privacy together.

Coda

37

It was barely dawn. The freeways were just filling up. Now it hit Jack how tired he was, but it was a "good tired." He had a feeling that something good had happened and by grace he had been a part if it. Immense gratification had come over him several times in the past, but never of this magnitude. Jack would never forget the look in Judy's eyes when she saw that her son could move his legs.

He was driving through familiar neighborhoods barely at the speed limit and savoring every minute of his triumphant ride. He felt like Roman emperors must have felt coming back to Rome for well-deserved parades after conquering foreign lands. His car felt like a quadriga, and he almost heard crowds on either side applauding him.

But then he landed back on earth and was thinking more about a good shower and a quiet breakfast. He would cancel his morning cases in the OR.

At home Diane was getting ready for a new day. She looked at Jack with a smile, her eyebrows raised slightly. Jack came closer, returned her smile, and gave her a hug. "Steven is OK." Tears rushed to her eyes.

"And how are you?"

"Ready for breakfast!"

Today he'd have no cases on the schedule. Tomorrow's were still on, but that was fine. Jack knew a tremendous weight had been lifted from his shoulders.

Outside perfect California weather extended blue and calm in every direction and the beautiful day was ahead. The sun was coming up from behind the Topatopa Mountains, and Jack felt there were no worries anywhere.

He was eagerly looking forward to spending time in the operating room tomorrow and the day after and then the next one.

Again.